Ivy couldn't fight it anymore. . . .

In the candlelight, Gregory's features cast rugged shadows. Golden light filled a little hollow in his neck. Ivy was tempted to touch that hollow, to lay her hand on his neck and feel where his pulse jumped.

"You know," Gregory said, "last winter, when my father told me he was marrying Maggie, the last thing I wanted was you in my house."

"I know," Ivy replied, smiling at him.

He reached out and touched her on the cheek.

"Now . . ." he said, spreading his fingers, letting them get tangled in her hair. "Now . . ." He pulled her head closer to his.

If we kiss, thought Ivy, if we kiss and—

"Now?" he whispered.

Ivy couldn't fight it anymore. She closed her eyes.

With both hands, Gregory pulled her face swiftly down to his.

Don't miss the other two books
in this exciting trilogy:

Volume I: *Kissed by an Angel*
Volume III: *Soulmates*

Available from ARCHWAY Paperbacks

KISSED BY AN ANGEL

THE POWER OF LOVE

Elizabeth Chandler

AN ARCHWAY PAPERBACK
Published by POCKET BOOKS
New York   London   Toronto   Sydney   Tokyo   Singapore

Lyric excerpts of "You'll Never Walk Alone," page 43, by Richard Rodgers and Oscar Hammerstein II. Copyright © 1945 by Williamson Music. Copyright renewed. International Copyright Secured. Used by Permission. All Rights Reserved.

This book is a work of fiction. Names, characters, places, and incidents are either products of the author's imagination or are used fictitiously. Any resemblance to actual events or locales or persons, living or dead, is entirely coincidental.

AN ARCHWAY PAPERBACK *Original*

An Archway Paperback published by
POCKET BOOKS, a division of Simon & Schuster Inc.
1230 Avenue of the Americas, New York, NY 10020

Produced by Daniel Weiss Associates, Inc., New York

Copyright © 1995 by Daniel Weiss Associates, Inc., and Mary Claire Helldorfer
Cover art copyright © 1995 by Daniel Weiss Associates, Inc.

ISBN: 0-671-89146-4

First Archway Paperback printing August 1995

10 9 8 7 6 5 4

AN ARCHWAY PAPERBACK and colophon are registered trademarks of Simon & Schuster Inc.

Printed in the U.S.A.

IL 7+

To the many hands that created this book.

1

"This time I'll reach her!" Tristan said. "I have to warn Ivy, I have to tell her that the crash *wasn't* an accident. Lacey, help me out! You know this angel stuff doesn't come naturally to me."

"You can say that again," Lacey replied, leaning back against Tristan's tombstone.

"Then you'll come with me?"

Lacey checked her nails, long purple nails that wouldn't chip or break any more than Tristan's thick brown hair would grow again. At last she said, "I guess I can squeeze in a pool party for an hour. But listen, Tristan, don't expect me to be a perfect, angelic guest."

Ivy stood at the edge of the pool, her skin prickling from the cold water that occasionally splashed her. Two girls brushed past her, chased by a guy with a water gun. The three of them tumbled into the pool together, leaving Ivy drenched by a shower of icy drops. If this had been the year before, she would have been trembling, trembling and praying to her water angel. But angels weren't real. Ivy knew that now.

The previous winter, when she had dangled from a diving board high above the school pool, frozen with a fear she had known since childhood, she had prayed to her water angel. But it was Tristan who had saved her.

He had taught her to swim. Though her teeth had chattered that first day and the next and the next, she had loved the feel of the water when he pulled her through it. She had loved him, even when he argued that angels weren't real.

Tristan had been right. And now Tristan was gone, along with her belief in angels.

"Going for a swim?"

Ivy turned quickly and saw her own suntanned face and tumbleweed of gold hair reflected in Eric Ghent's sunglasses. His wet hair was slicked back, almost transparent against his head.

"I'm sorry we don't have a high dive," Eric said.

She ignored the little jab. "It's a beautiful pool anyway."

2

"It's pretty shallow at this end," he said, pulling off his sunglasses, letting them dangle from their cord against his bony chest. Eric's eyes were light blue, and his lashes were so pale he looked as if he didn't have any.

"I can swim—either end," Ivy told him.

"Really." One side of Eric's mouth curled up. "Let me know when you're ready," he told her, then walked away to talk to his other guests.

Ivy hadn't expected Eric to be any nicer than that. Though he had invited her and her two closest friends to his midsummer pool party, they weren't members of Stonehill's fast crowd. Ivy was sure that Beth, Suzanne, and she were there only at the request of Eric's best friend and Ivy's stepbrother, Gregory.

She gazed across the pool at a line of sunbathers, searching for her friends. In the midst of a dozen oiled bodies and bleached heads sat Beth, wearing a huge hat and something resembling a muumuu. She was talking a mile a minute to Will O'Leary, another one of Gregory's friends. Somehow Beth Van Dyke, who had never even dreamed of being cool, and Will, who was thought to be ultracool, had become friends.

The girls around them were arranging themselves to show the sun—or Will—their best angle, but Will didn't notice. He was nodding encouragingly to

Beth, who was probably telling him her newest idea for a short story. Ivy wondered if, in his quiet way, Will enjoyed Beth's writings—poems and stories, and, once for history class, a biography of Mary, Queen of Scots—which somehow always turned into steamy bare-every-emotion tales of romance. The thought made Ivy smile.

Will glanced across the pool just then and caught the smile. For a moment his face seemed alight. Perhaps it was only the flicker of sun flashing off the water, but Ivy took a self-conscious step back. Just as quickly, he turned his face into the shade of Beth's hat.

As Ivy stepped back she felt the bare skin of a cool, hard chest. The person did not move out of the way, but rather lowered his face over her shoulder, brushing her ear with his mouth.

"I think you have an admirer," said Gregory.

Ivy did not move away from him. She had gotten used to her stepbrother, his tendency to lean too close, his way of showing up behind her unexpectedly. "An admirer? Who?"

Gregory's gray eyes laughed down at her. He was dark-haired, tall and slender, with a deep tan from spending hours a day playing tennis.

In the last month, he and Ivy had spent a lot of time together, though back in April she would never have believed it possible. Then, all that she and Gregory had in common was shock at their

4

parents' decision to marry, and anger at and distrust of each other. At seventeen, Ivy was earning her own money and looking after her kid brother. Gregory was racing around the Connecticut countryside in his BMW with a fast, rich crowd who scorned anyone who didn't have what they did.

But all that seemed unimportant now that he and Ivy had shared a lot more—the suicide of Gregory's mother and Tristan's death. When two people live in the same house, Ivy discovered, they share some of their deepest feelings, and, surprisingly enough, she had come to trust Gregory with hers. He was there for her when she missed Tristan the most.

"An admirer," Ivy repeated, smiling. "Sounds to me like you've been reading Beth's romances." She moved away from the pool, and Gregory moved with her like a shadow. Quickly Ivy scanned the patio area for her oldest and best friend, Suzanne Goldstein. For Suzanne's sake, Ivy wished Gregory would not stand so close. She wished he wouldn't whisper to her as if they shared some secret.

Suzanne had been pursuing Gregory since the winter, and Gregory had encouraged the chase. Suzanne said they were officially dating now; Gregory smiled and admitted to nothing. Just as Ivy laid a light hand on Gregory to push him back a little, a glass door slid open and Suzanne emerged from the pool house. She paused for a moment, as if taking in the scene—the long sapphire oval of the pool, the marble sculptures, the terraces of flowers. The pause conveniently gave all the guys a chance to look at her. With her shimmering mane of black hair and a tiny bikini that seemed more like jewelry than clothing, she outshone all the other girls, including the ones who had been longtime members of Eric and Gregory's crowd.

"If anyone has admirers," Ivy said, "it's Suzanne. And if you're smart, you'll get over there before twenty other guys line up."

Gregory just laughed and brushed back a tangle of golden hair from Ivy's cheek. He knew, of course, that Suzanne was watching. Both Gregory and Suzanne were into playing games, and Ivy was often caught in the middle.

Suzanne moved with catlike grace, reaching them quickly, yet never appearing to move faster than a leisurely stroll.

"Great suit!" she greeted Ivy.

Ivy blinked, then stared down at her one-piece in surprise. Suzanne had been with her when she bought the suit and had urged her to find something that plunged even further. But of course this was just a setup to turn Gregory's attention to Suzanne's . . . jewelry.

"It really looks terrific on you, Ivy."

6

"That's what I told her," Gregory said in an overly warm voice.

He had never said a thing about Ivy's suit. His white lie was intended to make Suzanne jealous. Ivy flashed him a look and he laughed.

"Did you bring any sunblock?" Suzanne asked. "I can't believe I forgot mine."

Ivy couldn't believe it, either. Suzanne had been working that line since they were twelve and vacationing at the Goldsteins' beach house.

"I know my back is going to fry," Suzanne said.

Ivy reached for her bag, which was on a nearby chair. She knew that Suzanne could stretch out on a sheet of foil at high noon and still never burn. "Here. Keep it. I've got plenty."

Then she placed the tube in Gregory's hands. She started off, but Gregory caught her by the arm. "How about you?" he asked, his voice low and intimate.

"How about me what?"

"Don't you need some lotion?" he asked.

"Nope, I'm fine."

But he wouldn't let her go. "You know how you forget the most obvious places," he said as he smoothed the lotion at the base of her neck and across her shoulders, his voice as silky soft as his fingers. He tried to slip a finger under one strap. Ivy held the strap down. She was getting

7

mad. No doubt Suzanne was burning up, too, she thought—though not from the sun.

Ivy pulled away from Gregory and quickly put on her sunglasses, hoping they would mask her anger. She walked away briskly, leaving them to tease and antagonize each other.

Both of them were using her to score points. Why couldn't they leave her out of their stupid games?

You're jealous, she chided herself. You're just jealous because they have each other, and you don't have Tristan.

She found an empty lounge chair at the edge of a small crowd and dropped down into it. The guy and girl next to her watched with interest as Suzanne led Gregory to two lounges in a corner apart from the others. They whispered as Gregory spread lotion over her perfectly shaped body.

Ivy closed her eyes and thought about Tristan, about their plans to run off to the lake together, to float out in the middle of it with the sun sparkling at their fingertips and toes. She thought about the way Tristan had kissed her in the backseat of the car the night of the accident. It was the tenderness of his kiss that she remembered, the way he had touched her face with wonder, almost reverence. The way he had held her made her feel not only loved, but sacred to him.

"You still haven't gone in the water."

8

Ivy opened her eyes. It seemed pretty clear that Eric wouldn't let her alone until she proved she would not freak out in the pool.

"I was just thinking about it," she said, removing her sunglasses. He waited for her by the pool's edge.

Ivy was glad that, at his own party, Eric had stayed sober. But perhaps this was how he made up for it. Without alcohol, without drugs, this was how Eric entertained himself: testing people on their most vulnerable points.

Ivy slipped into the water. In the first few moments the old fear washed over her as the water crept up her neck, and she was terribly afraid. "That's what courage is," Tristan had said, "facing what you're afraid of." With each stroke, she grew a little more comfortable.

She swam the length of the pool, then stopped and waited for Eric in the deep end. He was a poor swimmer.

"Not bad," Eric said when he caught up with her. "You're not bad for a beginner."

"Thanks," said Ivy.

"You're not even out of breath."

"I guess I'm in good shape."

"Not out of breath at all," he said. "You know, there's a game Gregory and I played at camp when we were little kids."

He paused, and Ivy guessed that he was going

9

to suggest they play it now. She wished they were hanging on to the wall at the other end of the pool, where it was shallow and the trees didn't crowd out the sun, and most everyone else now waded and sat.

"It's a test to see how long each of us can hold our breath," he told her. He spoke without looking at her; Eric rarely looked anyone in the eye.

"You have to duck under the water and stay under for as long as possible while the other person times it."

Ivy thought it was a dumb game, but she went along with it, figuring that the sooner they played it, the sooner she could get rid of him.

Eric quickly went under, holding his arm above the surface so she could read his watch. He stayed under for one minute and five seconds, surfacing with a rasping gasp. Then Ivy took a deep gulp of air and dropped down. She counted slowly to herself—one thousand one, one thousand two—determined to beat him. While she held her breath she watched her loose hair swirl around her. The chlorine was strong, and she wanted to close her eyes, but something told her not to trust Eric.

When she finally surfaced he said, "I'm impressed! One minute and three seconds."

She had counted one minute and fifteen.

"Here's the next step," he said. "We see if we

can stay under longer by going down together. It's like we encourage each other. Ready?"

Ivy nodded reluctantly. After this, she was getting out of the pool. Eric stared at his watch. "On the count of three. One, two—" He suddenly pulled her under.

Ivy hadn't gotten her breath. She pulled back, but Eric wouldn't let go. She waved her hands at him underwater but he gripped her upper arms.

Ivy began choking. Ivy had swallowed some water as Eric dragged her down, and she couldn't help coughing, trying to clear her lungs—but each time she did, she swallowed more water. Eric held her tight.

She tried to kick him but he moved his legs out of the way and smiled a close-lipped smile.

He's enjoying this, she thought. He thinks this is fun. He's crazy!

Ivy struggled to get away from him. Her stomach tightened with cramps, and her knees drew up. Her lungs felt as if they would burst.

Suddenly Eric grimaced. He pulled to one side so swiftly that he swung Ivy around with him. Then he let go. They both came to the surface, gasping and sputtering.

"You jerk. You stupid jerk!" Ivy yelled. But her coughing stopped her from going on.

Eric pulled himself up onto the wall, his face pale, his fingers still clutching his side. When his hand dropped, she saw the red marks, thin bloody stripes, as if someone had scratched his back and side with long, sharp fingernails.

Eric glanced around quickly with pale, unfocused eyes, then turned to her. His face seemed almost as distorted as it had underwater. "I was only playing," he said.

Someone called him from the opposite end of the pool. People were starting to move inside. He got up slowly and headed in the direction of the pool house. Ivy stayed by the side of the pool, taking deep breaths. She knew she had to stay in the pool. She had to wait till she was breathing normally again, then swim some laps. Tristan had led her past her fear. She was not going to let Eric take her back again. She began to swim.

When Ivy reached the end of the pool and made her turn for another lap, Beth reached down and grabbed her ankle. Ivy looked over her shoulder and saw Beth teetering on the edge of the pool, her large-brimmed hat coming down over her eyes. Will moved quickly to anchor Beth from behind.

"What's up?" Ivy asked, smiling at Beth, glancing quickly, self-consciously at Will.

"Everyone's going inside to watch videos," Beth told her enthusiastically, "some that were taken at school this year, and after school at basketball games and—" Beth stopped.

"Swim meets," Ivy finished the sentence for

her. Perhaps she could see, one more time, Tristan swimming the butterfly.

Beth took a step back from the edge of the pool and turned to Will. "I'm going to stay outside for a while."

"Don't stay outside for me, Beth," Ivy said. "I—"

"Listen," Beth interrupted her, "with everybody inside, I can finally bare this beautiful white bod and not worry about giving them all snow blindness."

Will laughed softly and said something intended for Beth's ears only.

Will was a sweet guy, but Ivy wouldn't have blamed him if he were furious at her, not after the scene she had made the previous Saturday night. He had drawn pictures of angels—one of Tristan as an angel with his arms wrapped around Ivy. She had ripped it to shreds.

"Go in and watch the videos, Beth," Ivy said firmly. "I just want to swim a little."

Will leaned forward then. "You shouldn't swim by yourself, Ivy."

"That's what Tristan used to say."

In response, Will gazed back at her with eyes that spoke a language of their own. They were brown pools, deep enough to drown in, Ivy thought. Tristan's had been hazel, and yet there was something similar about his eyes and Will's, something that drew her to him.

She turned away quickly, then caught her

13

breath. With a soft flash of colorful wings, a butterfly landed on her shoulder.

"A flyer," Beth said. Perhaps because they were all thinking about Tristan, Beth had used the word for a swimmer who did the butterfly.

Ivy tried to brush off the insect. Its wings fluttered, but it surprised her by staying put.

"It's mistaken you for a flower," Will said, smiling, his eyes full of light.

"Maybe," Ivy replied, anxious to get away from him and Beth. Pushing off from the side of the pool, she began to swim.

She did lap after lap, and when she was finally tired, she swam to the middle of the pool and flipped over to float.

"It's such a great feeling, Ivy. Do you know what it's like to float on a lake, a circle of trees around you, a big blue bowl of sky above you? You're lying on top of the water, sun sparkling at the tips of your fingers and toes."

The memory of Tristan's voice was so strong it was as if she heard it now. It seemed impossible that the big blue bowl of sky stayed up; it should have shattered like the car windshield the night of the accident, but there it was.

She remembered lying back in the water, feeling his arm beneath her as he taught her to float. "Easy now, don't fight it," he'd said.

She didn't fight it. She closed her eyes and imagined being in the center of a lake. When she had opened her eyes, he was looking down on her, his face like the sun, warming her.

"I'm floating," Ivy had whispered, and whispered it now.

"You're floating."

"Floating." They had read it off each other's lips, and for a moment now she felt as if he were bending over her still—"Floating"—their lips close, so close . . .

"Give 'em back!"

Ivy pulled her head up quickly, and her feet sank straight down beneath her. She quickly wiped the water out of her eyes.

The door of the pool house had been flung open, and Gregory was racing across the lawn, carrying a small piece of dark clothing in his hands. Odd globs of white, foamy stuff flew from his hair. Eric came streaking after him, one hand clutching Beth's hat—his only bit of cover—and the other wielding a long kitchen knife. "You're dead meat, Gregory."

"Come get them." Gregory egged him on, holding up Eric's trunks. "Come on. Give it your best shot."

"I'm going to—"

"Sure, sure," Gregory baited.

Eric suddenly stopped running. "I'll get you, Gregory," he warned. "When you least expect it."

15

2

Lacey sat back in the café chair, smiling at Tristan and looking very pleased with herself. Apparently she had forgiven him for dragging her away from the pool house free-for-all at Eric's party. Now she hooked her thumbs together and flapped her hands, rippling her fingers like wings. "You have to admit, landing that butterfly on Ivy was a nice touch."

Tristan eyed her shimmering fingers and long nails, and responded with something between a grimace and a smile. When he had first met Lacey Lovitt, he had thought the purple nails and the odd magenta rinse on her dark, spiked hair were a result of her hanging around in this world for two years—a long period of time for their kind of angel. But actually it was the way she liked her nails and hair to look, the way she had colored them after her last Hollywood film and before her plane went down.

"The butterfly was nice," he began, "but—"

"You're wondering how I did it," she interrupted. "I guess I'll have to teach you about using force fields." She eyed the dessert tray as it went by—not that she, or he, could actually eat.

"But—" Tristan said again.

"You're wondering how I knew about the butterfly," she said. "I told you, I read all about Stonehill High's hero, the great swimmer, Tristan Carruthers, in the local paper. I knew the butterfly was your stroke. I knew it would make Ivy think of you."

"What I was wondering was this: Couldn't you have left the pies alone?"

Her eyes slid over to the dessert tray again.

"Don't even think about it," he said.

There were only a handful of customers sitting at the town's outdoor café at four-thirty in the afternoon, but he knew Lacey could create chaos with very little. Two pies and some whipped cream—that's all it had taken earlier at Eric's. "I mean, isn't that kind of stunt a little old, Lacey? It was old when the Three Stooges did it."

"Oh, lighten up, Dumps," she replied. "Everyone at the party enjoyed it. Okay, okay," she said, "*some* people enjoyed it, and a few, like

Suzanne, got fussy about their hair. But *I* had a good time."

Tristan shook his head. Lacey had been lightning-quick, moving around the pool house, invisibly picking fights. She had obviously enjoyed yanking at Gregory's swimming trunks whenever Eric was close by. "Now I know why you never complete your mission," Tristan said.

"Well, *excu-u-use* me! *Please* remind me of that next time you *beg* me to come with you and help you reach Ivy." She stood up abruptly and stomped out of the café. Tristan was used to her dramatics and followed her slowly onto Main Street.

"You've got nerve, Tristan, criticizing my little bit of fun. Where were you when Ivy started making faces like a goldfish down in the deep end of the pool? Who took care of Eric?"

"You did," he said, "and you know where I was."

"All tangled up inside of Will."

Tristan nodded. The truth was embarrassing.

He and Lacey moved silently down the brick sidewalk, passing a row of shops with bright striped awnings. Windows full of antiques and dried-flower arrangements, art books and decorator wallpaper showed off the taste of the wealthy Connecticut town. Tristan still walked as if he were alive and solid, moving out of the way of shoppers. Lacey went straight through them.

"I must be doing something wrong," Tristan said at last. "One moment I'm inside Will, so much a part of him that when he looks at Ivy, I do, too. It's like he feels what I feel for her. Then all of a sudden he pulls back."

Lacey had stopped to look in the window of a dress shop.

"I must be pushing too hard," Tristan continued. "I need Will to speak for me. But I think he's discovered me prowling around in his mind, and now he's afraid of me."

"Or maybe," said Lacey, "he's afraid of *her*."

"Of Ivy?"

"Of his feelings for her."

"*My* feelings for her!" Tristan said quickly.

Lacey turned to look at him, her head cocked. Tristan feigned a sudden interest in an ugly black sequined dress hanging in the window. He couldn't see a reflection of Lacey's face in the glass, any more than he could see his own. Just a shimmer of gold and wisps of soft color shone against the window; he guessed that it was what a believer would see when looking at them.

"Why?" Lacey asked. "I want to know *why* you assume that you're the only guy in the world in love with—"

Tristan cut in. "I entered Will, and since he's a good radio, he started to feel my feelings and think my thoughts. That's how it works, right?"

"Didn't it ever occur to you that the reason it was so easy for an amateur like you to enter Will was because he was *already* feeling your feelings and thinking your thoughts, at least when it comes to Ivy?"

It had, but Tristan had done his best to squelch the idea.

"I got inside Beth's mind, too," he reminded her.

The first time Lacey had seen Beth, she had told Tristan that Ivy's friend would be a natural "radio," someone who could transmit messages from a different side of life. Just as Tristan had coaxed Will into drawing angels in an effort to comfort Ivy, he had gotten Beth to do some automatic writing, though it was so jumbled that no one had been able to make sense of it.

"You got inside, but it was tougher for you," Lacey pointed out. "You bumbled a lot, remember? And besides, Beth also loves Ivy."

She turned back to the window. "A killer dress," she said, then walked on. "What I really want to know is what everyone sees in this chick."

"It was nice of you to save a chick you think so little of," Tristan remarked dryly.

They passed the photo lab where Will worked and stopped in front of Celentano's, the pizza parlor where Will had drawn the angels on the paper tablecloth.

"I didn't save her," Lacey replied. "Eric was just playing—but you'd better figure out what kind of game it is. I've known some real creeps in my life, and I've got to say, he's not someone *I'd* like to party with."

Tristan nodded. He had so much to learn. After traveling back in time through his own mind, he was sure that someone had cut the brake line the night his car had slammed head-on into a deer. But he had no idea why.

"Do you think Eric did it?" he asked.

"Went after your brakes?" Lacey twisted a spike of purple hair around a daggerlike fingernail. "That's a leap, from being a bully in the deep end to committing murder. What did he have against you and Ivy?"

Tristan lifted his hands, then let them drop. "I don't know."

"What did anybody have against you or her? They could have been after just one of you. If it was you they wanted to get rid of, she's safe now."

"If she's safe, why was I brought back on a mission?"

"To annoy me," Lacey said. "Obviously you're some kind of penance for me. Oh, cheer up, Dumps! Maybe you just got your mission wrong."

She slipped through the door of Celentano's

without opening it, then reached up mischievously and jangled the three little bells over it. Two guys in T-shirts and grass-stained cutoffs stared at the door. Tristan knew she had materialized the tips of her fingers—a trick that he had just recently mastered—and managed to pull on the string of bells. She jangled them a second time, and the guys, unable to see either Lacey or Tristan, looked at each other.

Tristan smiled, then said, "You're going to scare away business."

Lacey climbed up on the counter next to Dennis Celentano. He had rolled out some dough and was expertly flipping it above his head—until it didn't come back down. It hung like a wet washrag in midair. Dennis gaped up at it, then leaned from one side to the other, trying to figure out what was holding up the dough.

Tristan guessed that the dough was going to be one more pie in the face. "Be nice, Lacey."

She dropped the dough neatly on the counter. They left Dennis and his customers to look at one another and wonder. "With you around," she complained to Tristan, "I'll be earning gold stars and finishing up my mission in no time."

Tristan doubted it. "Maybe you can earn some more stars by helping me with mine," he told her. "Didn't you tell me there was a way to travel back in time through somebody else's mind? Didn't you say I could search the past through someone else's memory?"

"No, I said *I* could," she replied.

"Teach me."

She shook her head.

"Come on, Lacey."

"Nope."

They were at the end of the street now, standing in front of an old church with a low stone wall around it. Lacey hopped up on the wall and began to walk it.

"It's too risky, Tristan. And I don't think it's going to help you any. Even if you could get inside a mind like Eric's, what do you think you'd find? That guy's circuits have been curled and fried. It could be—to use one of his terms—a very bad trip for you."

"Teach me," he persisted. "If I'm going to learn who cut the brakes, I'm going to have to go back to that night in the mind of everybody who might have seen something, including Ivy."

"Ivy! You'll *never* get in! That chick's got you and everyone else closed out cold."

Lacey paused, waiting till she had Tristan's full attention, then lifted up one leg as if she were doing a balance-beam routine. She's never lost her appetite for an audience, Tristan thought.

"I tried Ivy myself at the pool party this afternoon," Lacey went on. "I can't imagine how, even when you were alive, you and that chick ever got it on."

"Do you think you could come up with a way to give advice without making sarcastic remarks about 'that chick'?"

"Sure," she answered agreeably, and started walking the wall again. "But it wouldn't be half as much fun."

"I'll try Philip again," Tristan said, more to himself than to her. "And Gregory—"

"Now, *Gregory's* a tough nut to crack. Do you trust him? Stupid question," she said before he could answer. "You don't trust anyone who's got eyes for Ivy."

Tristan's head bobbed up. "Gregory's dating Suzanne."

She laughed down at him. "You're so naive! It's refreshing, for a jock-hunk type like you, but it's kind of pitiful, too."

"Teach me," he said for the third time, then reached up and caught her hand. Since angel hands did not pass through each other, he could hold on tight. "I'm worried about her, Lacey, I'm really worried."

She looked down at him.

"Help me."

Lacey stared at her long fingers caught by his.

25

She pulled her hand away very slowly, then reached down and patted him on the head. He hated the way she could patronize him, and he didn't like begging, but she knew things that would take a long time for him to learn on his own.

"Okay, okay. But listen up, because I'm only telling you once."

He nodded.

"First you have to find the hook. You have to find something that the person saw or did that night. The best kind of hook is an object or action that is connected with that night only, but avoid anything that might threaten your host. You don't want to set off alarm bells in his head."

She stepped carefully along a crumbling section of wall. "It's sort of like doing a word search on a library computer. If you pick a term that's too general, you'll call up all kinds of junk you don't want."

"Easy enough," he said with confidence.

"Uh-huh," she said, and rolled her eyes. "Once you've got your hook, you enter the person, like you've already done with Will and Beth, only you have to be more careful than ever. If your host feels you prowling around, if something feels strange to him, he's going to be on guard. Then he'll be too alert to let his mind wander back through memories."

"They'll never guess I'm there."

"*Uh-huh,*" she said again. "Be patient. Creep." She crept along the wall in slow motion. "And slowly bring into focus whatever image you're using for the hook. Remember to see it the same way that your host would."

"Of course." It was simple. He probably could have figured it out on his own, he thought. "And then?"

She jumped down from the wall. "That's it."

"That's it?"

"That's when the fun begins."

"But tell me what it's like, Lacey, so I know what to expect. Tell me how it feels."

"Oh, I think you probably could figure it out on your own."

He stopped short. "Can you read minds?"

She turned to look him straight in the eye. "No, but I'm pretty good at reading faces. And yours is like a large-print book."

He glanced away.

"You need me, Tristan, but you don't take me seriously. I met a lot of people like you when I was alive."

He didn't know what to say.

"Listen, I've got my own mission to work on. It's time I start poking around New York City, going back to the beginning and figuring out what I'm supposed to be figuring out.

Thanks to you, I'm already late for the train."

"Sorry," he said.

"I know you can't help it. Listen, if you should finish up your mission before I get back, can I have your grave? I mean, me not having one, unless you count my airplane seat at the bottom of the Atlantic, and you wouldn't be needing one after that—"

"Sure, sure."

"Of course, I might finish up my mission first."

After two years of procrastinating? he thought, but didn't dare say it aloud.

"I swear your face is like one of those large-print books my mother used to read."

Then she laughed and hurried off in the direction of the station that was at the edge of town, nestled between the river and the ridge.

Tristan turned the opposite way to climb a road that would take him to the top of the ridge, where the Baines house was. Philip might be home, he thought. Ivy's little brother had held on to the belief in angels that Ivy had given up. He could see Tristan shimmering, though he didn't know who it was. Strangely enough, Ivy's cat, Ella, saw Tristan, too.

He was able to pet Ella when he materialized the tips of his fingers. That was about as much as he could do now: pet a cat, pick up a piece of paper. Tristan longed to touch Ivy, to be strong enough to hold her in his arms.

He'd go straight to the house now and wait for her to come home from the party. He'd watch for Gregory, too. While he did, he'd figure out whose mind might hold the clue he needed—and how, please tell me how, he prayed, to reach Ivy!

3

Suzanne swatted back a piece of hanging plant that needed clipping, then stretched out luxuriously on her lounge. She wore a gold silk robe and had wrapped a green-and-gold towel around her head like a turban. Everything in the room—the large, round tub, the pillows, the luxurious carpeting and silk-grained wallpaper—was green or gold.

The first time Ivy had walked into this room at Suzanne's house, her eyes had popped open. She was seven years old then. The sumptuous bath, the elegant child's bedroom, and the velvet-lined trunks containing twenty-six Barbie dolls immediately convinced Ivy that Suzanne was a princess, and Suzanne didn't act otherwise. She was a remarkable princess who cheerfully shared all her toys and had a nice streak of wildness in her.

That day Ivy and Suzanne had snipped off small hunks of their own hair and made little wigs for the dolls. Twenty-six dolls required a lot of hair. Ivy figured she'd never get invited back, but soon she was being picked up by Mrs. Goldstein all the time, because Suzanne said she wanted to play with Ivy even more than she wanted her allowance or a pony.

Suzanne sighed, adjusted her turban, and opened her eyes. "Are you warm enough, Ivy?"

Ivy nodded. "Perfect." After bringing Suzanne home from the party, Ivy had changed from her wet bathing suit to a T-shirt and shorts. Suzanne had lent her a pink, satiny robe, which was needed in the air-conditioned house. It made Ivy feel like part of the princess scene.

"Perfect," Suzanne repeated, lifting a long, tan leg, pointing her toes. She took a sudden ungraceful swat at the plant hanging over her lounge, then dropped her leg and laughed. Now that the pie and whipped cream had been washed out of her hair, she was in a much better mood.

"He is . . . . perfect. Tell me the truth, Ivy," she said. "Does Gregory think about me often?"

"How would I know, Suzanne?"

Suzanne turned on her side to face Ivy. "Well, does Gregory talk about me?"

"He has," Ivy said cautiously.

"A lot?"

32

"Naturally he wouldn't say a lot to me. He knows I'm your best friend and would pass it along to you, or at least have it tortured out of me." Ivy grinned.

Suzanne sat up and whipped the towel off her head. A tumble of jet black hair fell over her shoulders.

"He's a flirt," she said. "Gregory will flirt with anyone—even you."

Ivy didn't take offense at the words *even you.* "Of course he will," she said. "He knows it gets to you. He likes to play games, too."

Suzanne dropped her chin and smiled up at Ivy through wisps of damp hair.

"You know," Ivy went on, "you two are supplying Beth with a ton of material. She'll have written five Harlequins before we graduate from high school. If I were you, I'd ask for a cut."

"Mmm." Suzanne smiled to herself. "And I've only just begun."

Ivy laughed and stood up. "Well, I've got to go now."

"You're going? Wait! We've hardly talked about the other girls at the party."

They had dissected the other girls all the way home, and shouted a dozen more catty comments over the loud drumming of Suzanne's shower.

"And we haven't talked about *you*," said Suzanne.

"Well, when it comes to me, there's really nothing to talk about," Ivy told her. She took off the robe and started folding it.

"Nothing? That's not what I heard," Suzanne said slyly.

"What did you hear?"

"Well, first off, I want you to know that when I heard it—"

"Heard what?" Ivy asked impatiently.

"—I told them all that, as someone who has known you a long time, I thought it unlikely."

"Thought what unlikely?"

Suzanne started combing her hair. "I may have even said *very* unlikely—I can't remember."

Ivy sat down. "Suzanne, what are you talking about?"

"At least I told them I was very surprised to hear that you were making out in the deep end with Eric."

Ivy's mouth dropped. "Making out with Eric! And you told them it was *unlikely?* More like totally impossible! Suzanne, you know I wouldn't!"

"I don't know anything for sure about you anymore. People do strange things when they're mourning. They get lonely. They try different ways to forget. . . . What exactly were you doing?"

34

"Playing a game."

"A kissing game?"

Ivy blew out through her lips. "A stupid game."

"Well, I'm glad to hear it," Suzanne said. "I don't think Eric's right for you. He's much too fast, and he plays around with some weird stuff. But of course you *should* start dating again."

"No."

"Ivy, it's time you started living again."

"Living and dating aren't the same thing," Ivy pointed out.

"They are to me," Suzanne replied.

They both laughed.

"What about Will?" Suzanne asked.

"What about him?"

"Well, he's kind of a newcomer to Stonehill, like you, and an artsy type—like you. Gregory said that the paintings he's entering in the festival are awesome."

Gregory had told Ivy the same thing. She wondered if the two of them were conspiring to get her and Will together.

"You're not still angry about him drawing those angels, are you?" Suzanne asked.

Drawing a picture of Tristan as an angel wrapping his arms around me, Ivy corrected silently. "I know he thought it would make me feel better," she said aloud.

"So cut him a break, Ivy. I know what you're thinking. I know exactly how you feel. Remember when Sunbeam died, and I said, 'That's it for Pomeranians. I never want another dog again'? But I've got Peppermint now and—"

"I'll think about it, okay?"

Ivy knew Suzanne meant well, but losing Tristan wasn't quite like losing a fourteen-year-old half-blind and completely deaf dog. She was tired of dealing with people who meant well and said ridiculous things.

Fifteen minutes later Ivy was headed home, her old Dodge climbing the long drive up the ridge. Several months earlier she would not have believed it possible, but she had grown fond of the low stone wall and the patches of trees and runs of wild flowers she passed—her stepfather Andrew's wall and trees and flowers. The large white house on top of the hill, with its wings and double chimneys and heavy black shutters, actually seemed like home now. The high ceilings did not look so high to her, the wide hall and center staircase no longer intimidated her, though she still usually scooted up the back steps.

It was about an hour before dinner and Ivy looked forward to some time by herself in her music room. It had been four weeks exactly since Tristan died—though no one else seemed to have noticed the date—and four weeks exactly since she had stopped playing the piano. Her nine-year-old brother, Philip, had begged her to play for him as she once did. But every time she sat down on the bench she went cold inside. The music was frozen somewhere within her.

I have to get past this block, Ivy thought as she pulled her car into the garage behind the house.

The Stonehill Arts Festival was two weeks away, and Suzanne had registered her as a performer. If Ivy didn't practice soon, she and Philip would have to do their famous "Chopsticks" duet.

Ivy paused outside the garage to watch Philip play beneath his tree house. He was so involved in his game, he didn't notice her.

But Ella did. It was as if the cat had been waiting for her, her green eyes wide and staring expectantly. She was purring even before Ivy rubbed her around her ears, her favorite spot, then she followed Ivy inside.

Ivy called hello to her mother and Henry, the cook, who were sitting at a table in the kitchen. Henry looked weary, and her mother, whose most complicated recipes were copied off soup cans, looked confused. Ivy guessed that they were planning another menu for a dinner entertaining benefactors of Andrew's college.

"How was the party, dear?" her mother asked.

"Good."

Henry was busily scratching items off Maggie's list. "Chicken à la king, chocolate pie with whipped cream," he said, sniffing with disapproval.

"See you later," Ivy said. When neither of them looked up, she headed for the back stairs.

The west side of the house, where the dining room, kitchen, and family room were, was the most-used section. A narrow gallery lined by pictures connected the family room to the wing occupied by Andrew's office on the first floor and Gregory's bedroom on the second. Ivy took the small staircase that ran up from the gallery, then crossed through the passage that led back into the main part of the house, into the hall with her room and Philip's. As soon as she entered her room she smelled something sweet.

She gasped with surprise. On her bureau, next to the photo of Tristan in his favorite baseball cap and old school jacket, were a dozen lavender roses. Ivy walked toward them. Tears rose quickly in her eyes, as if the salty drops had been there all along without her knowing.

Tristan had given her fifteen lavender roses the day after they argued about her belief in angels—one for each of her angel statues. When he saw how much she loved their unusual color, he'd bought her more, giving them to her on the way to a romantic dinner the night of the accident.

There was a note next to these roses. Gregory's jagged handwriting was never easy to decipher, and less so through tears. She wiped her eyes and tried again.

"I know these have been the hardest four weeks of your life," the note said.

Ivy lifted down the vase and laid her face lightly against the fragrant petals. Gregory had been there for her, looking out for her, since the night of the accident. While everyone else was encouraging her to remember that night and talk about the accident—because, they said, it would help her heal—he'd let her take her time, let her find her own way of healing. Perhaps it was his own loss, his mother's suicide, that had made him so understanding.

His note fluttered to the floor. Ivy quickly leaned over and picked it up. It fluttered down a second time. When she tried to pick it up again, the paper tore a little in her fingers, as if it had caught on something. Ivy frowned and gently smoothed the note. Then she set it back on the bureau, slipping one corner under the heavy vase.

Despite the tears, she felt more peaceful now. She decided to try playing the piano, hoping she'd be able to find the music within her. "Come on, Ella. Upstairs. I need to practice."

The cat followed her through a door in the

bedroom that hid a steep flight of steps leading to the house's third floor. Ivy's music room, which had a sloping roof and one dormer window, had been furnished by Andrew as a gift to her. It was still hard for Ivy to believe she had her own piano, a baby grand with gleaming, unchipped keys, kept perfectly in tune. She still marveled at the sound of the CD system, as well as the old-fashioned phonograph that could play the collection of jazz records that had belonged to her father.

At first Ivy had been embarrassed by the way Andrew lavished expensive gifts on both her and Philip. She had thought it angered Gregory. But now it seemed so long ago, those months when she'd thought that Gregory hated her for invading his life at home and school.

Ella scurried ahead of her into the room and leaped up on the piano.

"So, you're sure I'm going to play today," Ivy said.

The cat still had her wide-eyed look and stared just beyond Ivy, purring.

Ivy pulled out music books, trying to decide what to play. Anything, anything, just to get her fingers going. For the festival she would do something from one of her past recitals. As she sorted through classical scores she set aside a book of songs from Broadway musicals. That was the only kind of old, soft music that Tristan, a rock fan, had known.

She reached for Liszt and opened the score. Her hands trembled as they touched the smooth keys and she started her scales. Her fingers liked the familiar feel of the stretches; the repetitive rise and fall of notes soothed her. She glanced up at the opening measures of "Liebestraum" and willed herself to play. Her hands took over then, and it was as if she had never stopped playing. For a month she had been holding herself so tightly; now she gave in to the music that swirled up around her. The melody wanted to carry her, and she let it, let it take her wherever it would lead.

"I love you, Ivy, and one day you're going to believe me."

She stopped playing. The sense of him overwhelmed her. The memory was so strong—him standing behind her in the moonlight, listening to her play—that she could not believe he was gone. Her head fell forward over the piano. "Tristan! I miss you, Tristan!"

She cried as if someone had just now told her that he was dead. It will never get easier, she thought. Never.

Ella crowded close to her head, nosing her. When Ivy's tears stopped flowing, she reached for the cat. Then she heard a sound: three distinct notes. Ella's feet must have slipped, Ivy thought. She must have stepped down on the piano keys.

Ivy blinked back the wetness and cuddled the cat in her arms. "What would I do without you, Ella?"

She held the cat until she was breathing normally again. Then she set her gently on the bench and got up to wash her face. Ivy was halfway across the room, with her back to the piano, when she heard the same three notes again. This time the identical set of three was struck twice.

She turned back to the cat, who blinked up at her. Ivy laughed through a fresh trickle of tears. "Either I'm going crazy, Ella, or you've been practicing." Then she descended the stairs to her bedroom.

She wanted to pull the shades and sleep now, but she didn't let herself. She didn't believe the pain would ever lessen, but she had to keep going, keep focusing on the people around her. She knew that Philip had given up on her. He had stopped asking her to play with him three weeks ago. Now she'd go outside and ask him.

From the back door she saw him performing some kind of magic cooking ritual beneath two large maples and his new tree house. Sticks were arranged in a pile and an old crockpot sat on top.

It's only a matter of time, Ivy thought, before he decides to light one of these piles and sets fire to Andrew's landscaped yard. He had already done chalk drawings on the driveway.

She watched him with some amusement, and as she did the six notes floated back into her head. The repeated triplets were familiar to her, from some song she had heard long ago. Suddenly words attached themselves to the notes. "When you walk through a storm . . ."

Remembering the words slowly, Ivy sang, "When you walk through a storm . . . keep your head up high." She paused. "And don't be afraid of the dark." The song was from the musical *Carousel*. She couldn't recall much about the play except that at the end, a man who had died returned with an angel to someone he loved. The title of the song floated into her mind.

"'You'll Never Walk Alone,'" she said aloud.

She put her hand up to her mouth. She was going crazy, imagining Ella playing certain notes, imagining music with a message. Still, Ivy found some comfort in remembering that song.

Across the lawn Philip was chanting his own soft song over a pot of weedy greens. Ivy approached him quietly. When he looked up and waved a wand at her, she could tell he was making her a character in his game. She played along.

"Can you help me, sir?" she said. "I've been lost in the woods for days. I'm far from home, with nothing to eat."

"Sit down, little girl," Philip said in a quivery old-man voice.

Ivy bit her lip to keep from giggling.

"I will feed you."

"You're not—you're not a witch, are you?" she asked with dramatic caution.

"No."

"Good," she said, sitting down by the "campfire," pretending to warm her hands.

Philip carried the pot of leaves and weeds to her. "I'm a wizard."

"Eiii!" She jumped up.

Philip exploded with laughter, then quickly assumed his serious, wizardly look again. "I'm a good wizard."

"Phew!"

"Except when I'm mean."

"I see," said Ivy. "What's your name, wizard?"

"Andrew."

The choice took her aback for a moment, but she decided not to say anything about it. "Is that your house, Wizard Andrew?" she asked, pointing to the tree house above them.

Philip nodded.

The other Andrew, the one who did magic with his credit cards, had hired carpenters to rebuild the tree house Gregory had played in as a child. It was more than doubled in size now, with a narrow boardwalk leading to the maple next to it, where more flooring and railings had been hammered into place. In both trees, upper levels had been added. A rope ladder dangled from one maple, and a thick rope that ended in a knot beneath a swing seat hung from the other. It was everything a kid could want, and more—Gregory and Ivy had agreed on that after climbing around in it one day when Philip was out.

"Do you want to come up to my hideout?" Philip asked her now. "You'll be safe from all the wild beasts, little girl."

He scampered up the rope ladder and Ivy followed, enjoying the physical effort, the hard rub of the rope against her palms, and the way the wind and her own motion made the ladder sway. They climbed up two levels from the main floor, then stopped to catch their breath.

"It's nice up here, Wiz."

"It's safe," Philip replied. "Except when the silver snake comes."

Fifty yards beyond them was the low stone wall marking the end of the Baines property. From there, the earth dropped away steeply into a landslide of jagged rocks, tangled scrub, and spindly trees that bent in odd ways to keep their hold in the rocky ground. Far below the Baines property was Stonehill's tiny railroad station, but from the tree house one could hear only the whistles of the trains as they ran between the river and the ridge.

Farther to the north, Ivy could see a twisting piece of blue, like a ribbon cut from the sky and dropped between the trees, and, next to it, a train crawling along, flashing back the sunlight.

She pointed to it. "What's that, Wizard Andrew?"

"The silver snake," he replied without hesitation.

"Will it bite?"

"Only if you stand in its way. Then it will gobble you up and spit you out in the river."

"Ugh."

"Sometimes at night it climbs up the ridge," Philip said, his face absolutely serious.

"It couldn't."

"It does!" he insisted. "And you have to be very careful. You can't make it angry."

"Okay, I won't say a word."

He nodded approvingly, then warned, "You can't let it know you're afraid. You have to hold your breath."

"Hold my breath?" Ivy studied her brother.

"It will see you if you move. It watches you

46

even when you don't think it's watching. Day and night."

Where was he getting this stuff from?

"It can smell you if you're afraid."

Was he really frightened of something, or was this just a game? she wondered. Philip had always had an active imagination, but it seemed to her it was becoming overactive and darker. Ivy wished his friend Sammy would return from summer camp. Her brother had everything he could want now, but he was too isolated from other kids. He was living too much in his own world.

"The snake won't get me, Philip," she told him, almost sternly. "I'm not afraid of it. I'm not afraid of anything," she said, "because we're safe in our house. All right?"

"All right, little girl, you stay here," he said. "And don't let anyone else in. I'm going over to my other house and get some magic clothes for you. They will make you invisible."

Ivy smiled a little. How would she play invisible? Then she picked up a battered broom and began to sweep off the flooring.

Suddenly she heard Philip yelp. She spun around and saw him tottering on the edge of the narrow boardwalk, sixteen feet above the ground. She dropped the broom and rushed toward him, but knew she couldn't catch him in time.

Then, just as suddenly, he was balanced again.

He dropped down on all fours and looked back over his shoulder. The rapt expression on his face stopped Ivy in her tracks. She had seen that look on his face before: the wonder, the glow of pleasure, his mouth half open in a shy smile.

"What happened?" Ivy asked, moving toward him slowly now. "Did you trip?"

He shook his head, then picked up the loose end of a board.

Ivy leaned down to study it. The bridge had been constructed like a miniature boardwalk, with two long, thin boards secured between the two trees and a series of short planks laid across them. The short planks overhung the boards a few inches on each side. This particular plank was nailed loosely on one side—Ivy could pull the nail out with her hands; on the other side there was a hole, but no nail.

"When I stepped here"—Philip pointed—"the other side came up."

"Like a seesaw," said Ivy. "It's a good thing you didn't lose your balance."

Philip nodded. "Good thing my angel was right here."

Ivy sucked in her breath.

" 'Cause sometimes he isn't. Though he usually is when you're around."

Ivy closed her eyes and shook her head.

"He's gone now," said Philip.

Good, thought Ivy. "Philip, we've talked about this before. There are no such things as angels. All you have is a bunch of statues—"

"Your statues," he interrupted. "I'm taking good care of them."

"I told you," she said, her throat tightening and her head starting to throb, "I told you that if you wanted to keep those statues, you must never speak to me about angels again. Didn't I tell you that?"

He lowered his head and nodded.

"Didn't you promise?"

He nodded again.

Ivy sighed and pulled up the piece of wood. "Now slide around behind me. Before you go any farther, I want to check each board."

"But, Ivy," he said, "I saw my angel! I saw him catch the wood on the other side and push it down so I wouldn't fall. I saw him!"

Ivy sat back on her heels. "Don't tell me. Let me guess. He was wearing wings and a nightgown, and had a little saucer of light on his head."

"No, he was just light. He was just shining. I think he has sort of a shape, but it's always hard for me to see it. It's hard for me to see his face," Philip said. His own young face was earnest.

"Stop it!" said Ivy. "Stop it! I don't want to hear any more about it! Save it for when Sammy gets home, okay?"

"Okay," he said, the corners of his mouth stiff and straight. He slipped past her.

Ivy began to examine the boards and could hear her brother sweeping the tree house behind her. Then the broom stopped. She glanced over her shoulder. Philip's face was happy and bright again. He still clutched the broom, but he was standing on his tiptoes, stretching upward. "Thank you," he mouthed silently.

4

That evening Ivy wandered from room to room in the house, feeling restless and edgy. She didn't want to go out or call up a friend, but she could find nothing to do at home. Each time she heard the clock chime in the dining room, she couldn't stop her mind from turning back to the night Tristan died.

When Maggie and Andrew went to bed, Ivy went up to her room to read. She wished that Gregory were home. In the last few weeks they had watched a lot of late-night TV together, sitting quietly side by side, sharing cookies, laughing at the dumb jokes. She wondered where he was now. Maybe he had helped Eric clean up after the party, then the two of them had gone out. Or maybe he had gone to Suzanne's. She could call Suzanne and say—Ivy caught herself before that thought went any further. What was she thinking? Call up Suzanne in the middle of a date?

I depend on Gregory way too much, Ivy thought.

She crept downstairs and took a flashlight from the kitchen drawer. Maybe a walk would make her sleepy; maybe it would get rid of that prickling feeling in the back of her mind. When Ivy opened the back door, she saw Gregory's BMW parked outside the garage. He must have brought back the car at some point and taken off again. She wished he were there to walk with her.

The driveway, a continuous curve down the side of the ridge, was three quarters of a mile long. Ivy walked it to the bottom. After the steep climb back, her body finally felt tired, but her mind was still awake and as restless as the tossing trees. It was as if there was something she had to remember, and she couldn't sleep until she remembered it—but she had no idea what it was.

When she arrived back at the house, the wind had changed and a sharp, wet smell swept over the ridge. In the west, lightning flashed, casting up images of clouds like towering mountains. Ivy longed for a storm with bright lightning and wind to release whatever it was that was pent up inside her.

At one-thirty she climbed into bed. The storm

had skirted their side of the river, but there were more flashes in the west. Maybe they would get the next big gust of rain and wind.

At two o'clock she was still awake. She heard the long whistle of the late-night train as it crossed the bridge and rushed on through the little station far below the house. "Take me with you," she whispered. "Take me with you."

Her mind drifted after the lonely sound of the whistle, and Ivy felt herself slipping away, rocked by the low rumbling of thunder in the distant hills.

Then the rumbling became louder, louder and closer. Lightning quivered. The wind gusted up, and the trees that had been slowly swaying from side to side now lashed themselves with soaked branches. Ivy peered out through the storm. She could hardly see, but she knew something was wrong. She opened a door.

"Who is it?" she cried out. "Who's there?"

She was outside now, struggling against the wind and moving toward a window, with lightning streaking all around her. The window was alive with reflections and shadows. She could barely make out the figure on the other side, but she knew something or someone was there, and the figure seemed familiar to her.

"Who is it?" she called out again, moving closer and closer to the window.

She had done this before, she knew she had, sometime, somewhere, perhaps in a dream, she thought. A feeling of dread washed over her.

She *was* in a dream, caught in it, the old nightmare. She wanted out! Out!

She knew it had a terrible end. She couldn't remember it, only that it was terrible.

Then Ivy heard a high whining sound. She spun around. The sound increased till it drowned out the storm. A red Harley roared up to her.

"Stop! Please stop!" Ivy cried. "I need help! I need to get out of this dream!" The motorcyclist hesitated, then gunned his engine and sped off.

Ivy turned back to the window. The figure was still there. Was it beckoning to her? Who or what could it be? Ivy put her face close to the window. Suddenly the glass exploded. She shrieked and shrieked as the bloody deer came crashing through.

"Ivy! Ivy, wake up!"

Gregory was shaking her. "Ivy, it's just a dream. Wake up!" he commanded. He was still fully dressed. Philip stood behind him, a little ghost in pale pajamas.

Ivy looked from one to the other, then sagged against Gregory. He put his arms around her.

"Was it the deer again?" Philip asked. "The deer coming through the window?"

Ivy nodded and swallowed hard several times.

It was good to feel Gregory's arms strong and steady around her. "I'm sorry I woke you up, Philip."

"It's okay," he said.

She tried to still her trembling hands. Gregory's home now, she told herself, everything's okay.

"I'm sorry this keeps happening, Philip. I didn't mean to scare you."

"I'm not scared," he replied.

Ivy glanced up sharply at her brother's face and saw that, in fact, he wasn't.

"The angels are in my room," he explained.

"Then why don't you go back to them?" Gregory told him. Ivy felt the tightening muscles in his arms. "Why don't you—"

"It's all right, Gregory. Let Philip alone," she said with soft resignation. "He's dealing with this the best way he can."

"But he's making it harder on you," Gregory argued. "Can't you understand, Philip? I've tried a million times to—"

He stopped, and Ivy knew that Gregory saw it, too: the brightness in Philip's eyes, the certainty in his face. For a moment the little boy's will seemed stronger than both of theirs put together. It was impossible to argue him out of what he believed. Ivy found herself wishing that she could be so innocent again.

Gregory sighed and said to Philip, "I can take

care of Ivy. Why don't you get some shut-eye? We've got a big day tomorrow—the Yankees game, remember?"

Philip glanced at Ivy and she nodded in agreement.

Then he gazed past her and Gregory in such a way that she instinctively turned around to look. Nothing.

"You'll be okay," he said confidently, and trotted off to bed.

Ivy sank back against Gregory. He wrapped his arms around her again. His hands were gentle and comforting. He brushed back her hair, then lifted her face up to his.

"How are you doing?" he asked.

"All right, I guess."

"You can't shake that dream, can you?"

She saw his concern. She saw how he searched her face for clues about what she was feeling.

"It was the same dream but different," Ivy told him. "I mean, there were things added to it."

His frown of worry deepened. "What was added?"

"A storm. There were all those mixed-up images on the window again, but this time I realized it was a storm I was seeing. The trees were blowing and lightning was flashing and reflecting off the glass. And there was a motorcycle," she said.

It was hard for her to explain the nightmarish

feeling the motorcycle gave her, for that part of the dream was simple and ordinary. The motorcyclist had not harmed her. All he had done was refuse to stop to help her.

"A red motorcycle came rushing by," she continued. "I called out to the rider, hoping he would help me. He slowed down for a moment, then kept on going."

Gregory held her face against his chest and stroked her cheek. "I think I can explain that. Eric just dropped me off. He has a red Harley—you've seen it before. You must have heard the sound of it while you were sleeping and woven it into your dream."

Ivy shook her head. "I think there's more to it than that, Gregory," she said quietly.

He stopped stroking her cheek. He held very still, waiting for her to go on.

"Remember how it was storming the evening your mother ki—died?"

"Killed herself," he said clearly.

She nodded. "And I was in the neighborhood then, making a delivery for the store."

"Yes."

"I think that's part of the dream. I had completely forgotten about it. I had thought my nightmare was just about Tristan and the accident, with the deer crashing through the glass, crashing through our windshield. But it's not."

She paused and tried to sort things out in her mind.

"For some reason I put the two events together. The night your mother died, I couldn't find the right house. When I got out to check a street sign, someone on a red motorcycle came by. He saw me flagging him down and hesitated, but then rushed on past me."

She could feel Gregory's steady, rapid breathing on her forehead. He held her so close, she could hear the quick beat of his heart.

"Later I thought I had found the house—I had narrowed it down to two houses. One of them had a big picture window, and someone was standing inside, but I couldn't see who it was. I thought it might be the person who was waiting for my delivery. Then the door to the house next door opened—and that's where I was supposed to be."

It was strange the way the details of that night were slowly coming back to her.

"Don't you see, Gregory? That's the window I keep coming up to in the dream and trying to see through. I don't know why."

"Do you know if it was Eric you saw that night?" he asked.

Ivy shrugged. "It was a red motorcycle, and the rider had a red helmet. But then, I guess a lot of people do. If it had been Eric, wouldn't he have stopped for me?"

Gregory didn't answer.

"Maybe not," said Ivy. "I mean, I know he's your friend, but he's never really liked me," she added quickly.

"As far as I know," Gregory said, "Eric's really liked only one person in his life. He can make things very hard for the people around him."

Ivy glanced up, surprised. Gregory saw Eric more clearly than she had realized. Still, he had remained a loyal friend to him, just as he was a friend to her now.

She relaxed against him. She was getting sleepy now, but was reluctant to pull away from the comfort of his arms.

"Isn't it strange," Ivy mused, "that I should put your mother's death and Tristan's together in one dream?"

"Not really," Gregory replied. "You and I have been through a lot of pain, Ivy, and we've been through it together, helping each other get by. It seems pretty natural to me that you would link those events in your dream." He lifted her face to his once again, looking deeply into her eyes. "No?"

"I guess so," she said.

"You really miss him, don't you? You can't help but keep remembering."

Ivy dropped her head, then smiled up at him through her tears. "I'll just have to keep remembering how lucky I am to have found a friend like you, someone who really understands."

"This is better than any flick coming out of Hollywood this summer," Lacey said.

"Who invited you in here?" Tristan asked.

He had been sitting by Ivy's bed watching her sleep—he didn't know for how long. At last Gregory had left him alone with her. At last Ivy looked at peace.

After Gregory left, Tristan had sorted through what he'd learned, and tried hard to keep himself conscious. The dreamless darkness had not come upon him for a while now. It did not come upon him as swiftly and as often as when he first became an angel, but he knew he could not keep going without rest. Still, as tired as he was, he could not bear to give up these moments alone with Ivy in the quiet of the night. He resented Lacey's intrusion.

"I was sent by Philip," she told him.

"By Philip? I don't understand."

"In Manhattan today I found this funky guardian angel statue, a baseball player with wings." She flapped her arms dramatically. "I got it for him as a little gift."

"You mean you stole it?"

"Well, how would you like me to pay for it?" she snapped. "Anyway, I was just dropping it off.

60

He saw my glow and pointed, directing me in here. I guess he figured his sister needed all the help she could get."

"How long have you been here?" Tristan asked. He hadn't noticed Lacey's arrival.

"Ever since Gregory brushed back her hair and lifted her face up to his," she replied.

"You saw that?"

"I tell you, Hollywood could use him," Lacey said. "He's got all the right moves."

Lacey's view was both welcome and frightening to Tristan. On the one hand, he wanted Gregory to be doing nothing more than playing a romantic game with Ivy; he didn't want anything real to be happening between them. On the other hand, Tristan feared that there could be a darker reason behind such a game.

"So you heard it all. You've been here all this time."

"Yep." Lacey climbed up on the headboard of Ivy's bed. Her brown eyes glinted like shiny buttons, and her spikes of purple hair were pale and feathery in the moonlight. She perched above Ivy's head.

"I didn't want to disturb you. You were so deep in thought," she said. "And I figured you wanted time alone with her."

Tristan cocked his head. "Why are you suddenly being so thoughtful? Have you finished your mission? Are you getting ready to leave?"

"Finished?" She almost choked on the word. "Uh . . . no," she said, glancing away from him. "I doubt I'll be shoving off to the next realm anytime soon."

"Oh," he said. "So, what happened in New York?"

"Uh . . . I don't think I should tell you. It'll probably be in the papers tomorrow, anyway."

Tristan nodded. "So you're earning back a few points now."

"Take advantage of me while you can," she urged.

Tristan smiled.

"I get points for that," she said, just touching his lips with the tip of a long nail, but his smile had already disappeared. "You're really worried."

"You heard the dream," he said. "It's pretty obvious. There's some connection between Caroline's death and mine."

"Tell me about Caroline. How'd she croak?" Lacey asked.

"Shot herself, in the head."

"And they're sure it was a suicide?"

"Well," said Tristan, "the police found only her fingerprints on the gun, and her fingers were still twisted around it. She left no note, but she had torn up photographs of Gregory's father and Ivy's mother."

Lacey sprang off the headboard and began to pace the room in a circle.

"I suppose someone could have set it up to look like a suicide," Tristan said slowly. "And Ivy was in the neighborhood that night. She could have seen something. Lacey! What if she saw something she shouldn't have—"

"Did I ever tell you I was in *Perry Mason?*" Lacey interrupted.

"—and what if she didn't even realize it?" Tristan exclaimed.

"Of course, Raymond Burr is dead now," Lacey continued.

"I need to check out the address of Gregory's mother," Tristan told her, "and the address where Ivy made the delivery that night."

"As soon as I read the obit, I looked Raymond up," Lacey said.

"Listen to me, Lacey."

"I was sure he would be assigned some kind of mission."

"Lacey, please," he begged.

"I thought we could pal around together."

"Lacey!" he shouted.

"I mean, Raymond would make an awesome angel."

Tristan dropped his head in his hands. He needed time to think about what was going on and how he could keep Ivy safe.

"But he must have whisked right on," Lacey said.

"Must have," Tristan mumbled. He could feel

63

his mind growing dim. He needed rest before he could figure things out.

"I can't tell you how disappointed I was!"

"You just did," Tristan observed wearily.

"Raymond said he'd never forget the episode I did with him."

There could be a lot of reasons for that, Tristan thought.

"Raymond always appreciated my talent."

Ivy was in danger, and he didn't know how to warn her or whom to warn her against, and Lacey was going on and on about a dead actor.

"So what I am saying is that I can probably help you on this matter," Lacey said.

Tristan stared at her. "Because you played a supporting role in one episode with another actor who pretended he was a lawyer who somehow ended up solving television crimes?"

"Well, if you're going to put it that way, don't expect my help!"

She stalked across the room, then paused theatrically and looked over her shoulder.

Tristan wished she'd keep right on going. The room was washed in the palest of morning light now, and the first birds were up, their flickering song being passed along from one tree to the next. He wanted the last bit of time he could have alone with Ivy. He turned toward her, longing to touch her.

"I wouldn't do that if I were you."

"You don't know what I'm going to do," Tristan replied.

"Oh, I can guess," she said to his back. "And you're too exhausted."

"Leave me alone, Lacey."

"I just thought I'd warn you."

"Leave me alone!"

She did.

As soon as she left he stretched out his hand. Ivy slept quietly beneath it. He wanted so badly to touch her, to feel her warmth, to know her softness just one more time. Gathering all his strength, Tristan focused on the tips of his fingers. He knew he was tired, too tired, but still he concentrated with his last bit of energy. The ends of his fingers stopped shimmering. They were solid now.

Slowly, gently, he ran his fingers down her cheek, feeling the silk of her, the wonder of her. He traced Ivy's mouth.

If only he could kiss those lips! If only he could hold Ivy, fold all of her in his arms . . .

Then he began to lose the sense of her.

He reached again, but he was losing touch. "No!" he cried out. It felt like he was dying all over again. The pain of losing her was so intense, so unbearable, that when the dreamless darkness came, he gave himself over to it willingly.

5

"Well, hello, sleepyhead," said the girl sitting on the mall bench.

Tristan jumped, startled out of deep thought. He had emerged from the darkness about fifteen minutes before and immediately tracked Ivy to her job at 'Tis the Season. For the last few minutes he'd been trying to piece together the fragments of Ivy's dream and what those pieces meant, but his mind still felt dark and muddled.

Lacey laughed at him. "Know what day it is?"

"Uh, Monday."

"*Brrtt.*" She did her obnoxious imitation of a game-show buzzer, then gestured to the seat next to her.

Tristan sat down. "It's Monday," he insisted. "When I came into the mall, I checked a newspaper, just like you told me to do."

"Maybe you should have checked the *latest* one," Lacey observed. "It's Tuesday, and nearly one o'clock. Ivy should be taking her break soon."

He looked across the mall toward the shop. Ivy was busy with two customers, a bald old man trying on a Superman cape and a grandmotherly type holding a pink basket and wearing bunny ears. He knew that 'Tis the Season sold costumes and holiday items—most of which were out of season. But the recent darkness, the two customers in their odd outfits, and the presence of a very large woman carrying a bagel and coffee who had just sat down on Tristan made it all very confusing.

Lacey patted his arm. "I told you that you were too tired. I warned you."

"Move over," he grunted. He couldn't feel the woman's weight, but it seemed a little weird having her wide, striped dress flowing over him.

Lacey slid down a little and said, "I have something to tell you. While you were in the darkness, I've been busy."

"I already know."

The Monday paper had caught his attention because of an article on people gathering to pray in Times Square after an image of Barbra Streisand, projected on an electronic billboard,

68

grew a chubby, pink angel body and flitted around.

"Does this have anything to do with the traffic jams on Forty-second Street?" he asked.

She dismissed the event with a wave of her hand.

"I read something about Streisand considering a lawsuit, and how the New York cabbies—"

"Barbra should never have said I honked like a goose. Not that I couldn't have used a few more voice lessons—"

"Lacey, how are you ever going to complete your mission?"

"My mission? Today I'm helping you with yours," she said, then sprang up from the bench.

Tristan shook his head and followed her.

"I went to the cemetery Sunday to pay a visit to Gregory's mother," Lacey said as they walked along with the shoppers. "While I was there, somebody came by, a tall, thin guy, dark-haired. About forty, I think. He left Caroline some flowers."

"He's been there before," Tristan said. "I saw him the day we were in the chapel." He remembered watching the visitor from behind, mistaking him for Gregory until he turned around. He could still see the man's face, full of anguish.

"What's his name?" she asked.

"I don't know."

They were heading away from 'Tis the Season. Tristan looked back longingly at Ivy, but Lacey marched on.

"We should find out. He might be able to help us."

"Help us what?" Tristan asked.

"Figure out what happened the night Caroline died."

They stopped by the fountain to watch cascades of water fall in pink and blue drops. One day, when nobody was looking, Tristan had made a wish here, a wish that Ivy would be his.

"I looked up Caroline's address in the phone book," Lacey went on. "Five twenty-eight Willow. Her date of death was written on her tombstone. I came here this morning to check out the shop records for that day." She paused and looked at Tristan expectantly.

When he didn't say anything, she said, "What an angel you are, Lacey, helping me out like this."

"What did you find out?" he asked, ignoring her sarcasm.

"For one thing, that Lillian and her sister haven't a clue about how to keep business books. But after a lot of hunting and squinting I did find it: a delivery on May twenty-eighth to a Mrs. Abromaitis on Willow Street—no house number given. I looked it up in the phone book. Guess what? Five thirty Willow."

"Right next door," Tristan said, his voice a whisper, his mind prickling with fear. "I knew it. Ivy saw something."

"Looks that way," Lacey agreed. She caught a coin that a woman had tossed toward the fountain and flipped it back at her. The woman stared down at it, then stuck the unlucky penny in a pot of ferns.

"Ivy saw something at Caroline's," Tristan said, "and it wasn't a suicide."

"We can't assume that," Lacey replied. "Caroline still could have killed herself, and someone could have been there afterward, taking something or hiding something. I mean, there are a lot of things Ivy could have seen—"

"That she shouldn't have," Tristan finished Lacey's sentence. "I have to reach her, Lacey!"

"I thought we should check out the house today."

"I have to warn her now!"

"I remember how we did a search on *Perry Mason*," Lacey said. She started pulling Tristan toward the mall exit, but he was intent on heading back to 'Tis the Season, and he was stronger. "Tristan, listen to me! There's nothing you can do to protect Ivy. You and I weren't given that kind of power. The best you can do is combine the powers you do have with someone else and make that person stronger. But you yourself can't stop anyone who wants to harm her."

Tristan stood still. He had never feared for his own life the way he now feared for Ivy's.

"As long as she's in a crowd, she's safe," Lacey added. "So let's check out the house and—"

"As soon as she gets in her car tonight, she'll be alone," Tristan pointed out. "As soon as she goes for a walk, as soon as she goes up to her music room, she'll be in danger."

"There are other people at home with her," Lacey pointed out. "She's probably safe there. So let's find out who she has to watch out for and then—"

But Lacey was left to talk to herself. Beth and Suzanne had just entered the mall. Spotting them, Tristan turned quickly and began to walk with them. He figured they were meeting Ivy for lunch. This time he would get through.

Ivy was standing by the shop entrance, and for a moment Tristan forgot she was seeing only the girls. When he saw the look of welcome on her face, he hurried toward her, only to find she was now looking past him at Suzanne and Beth. It never got easier—the pain of being close to her, but far away, never seemed to lessen.

"Now, take your time over lunch," Lillian was saying to the girls. "It's a slow day, so do a little shopping. Be sure to take a peek in that new gift shop. I'll bet *they* don't have glow-in-the-dark wind chimes."

"Not in the shape of leprechauns and fairies," Beth said. Whenever she came to the shop, she got a look of total wonder on her face. Suzanne had to reach back and pull her out the door.

Tristan followed the girls through the mall. They stopped at one store window after another, and he began to grow impatient. He wanted Beth to sit down right away and start scribbling in her notebook. He thought they'd never get out of the Beautiful You shop, with all those bottles and tubes and little pots of color.

He began to pace from one side of the store to the other and ran head-on into Lacey. He hadn't realized that she had come along.

"Chill out, Tristan," Lacey said. "Ivy's safe for now, unless someone runs her through with a nail file."

Then she wandered off to a corner, as mesmerized as the others by the hundreds of colors— which all looked pretty much like red and pink to him. Tristan wondered whether, if he ever made it to the next realm, some mysteries about girls would be explained.

Suzanne, now wearing stripes of tester lipstick all the way up her arm, was talking about a wedding in Philadelphia that she was going to that weekend.

"I wish you were coming with us, Ivy," she said. "I showed my cousin your picture. He's definitely interested, and he's so perfect for you."

Terrific, thought Tristan.

"So you decided to go to the lake after all?" Beth asked. She was trying on a shower cap that looked like a silver mushroom.

"The lake!" Suzanne said, surprised. "She's staying home, and you're staying with her, Beth."

Beth frowned. "Suzanne, you know I can't miss my family reunion. I thought she was going to Philly with you."

Ivy had turned away from both of them.

"Ivy!" Suzanne commanded.

"What?" She started sorting through a bin of barrettes and didn't look up.

"What are you doing this weekend?"

"Staying home."

Suzanne raised her perfectly shaped black eyebrows. "Your mother's letting you stay alone?"

"She thinks that you and Beth will be with me. And I'm counting on you two to cover for me," Ivy added.

Lacey glanced over at Tristan.

"I don't know what the big deal is," Ivy went on. "I'd like to have the house to myself for a change. I'll have plenty of time to practice for the festival, and Ella will keep me company."

"But Ella can't protect you," Tristan protested.

"I just don't like the idea of you moping around all weekend by yourself," Suzanne said.

"That house is too big, too lonely," Beth added.

"Listen to them, Ivy," Tristan urged.

"I told you both, I won't go to Juniper Lake! I can't!"

"This is some kind of Tristan thing, isn't it?" Suzanne said.

"I don't want to talk about it," Ivy replied.

It was. Tristan remembered the plans they had made the night he died. Ivy had told him how she was going to float in the sunlight in the deepest part of Juniper Lake. "I'll swim in the moonlight, too."

"The moonlight?" he'd said. "You'd swim in the dark?"

"With you I would."

Lacey touched Tristan on the arm. "You've got to get through to her this time."

He nodded.

They followed the girls out of the store. Tristan was tempted to slip inside Beth's mind right then, to direct her toward a table where she could take out her writing pad, but he didn't want to give her too many instructions. She might begin to resist.

Beth stopped suddenly in front of Electronic Wizard, and Tristan followed her eyes to a display of computers inside.

"Look at her. Look at her!" Suzanne said, nudging Ivy. "You'd think Beth was checking out guys."

"There's the laptop I want," Beth said.

Then Lacey came up quickly behind her. Tristan saw that the tips of her fingers had stopped shimmering. She gave a swift push. Beth stumbled through the door and looked back in surprise at Suzanne and Ivy. They followed Beth inside, with Tristan and Lacey right behind them.

"Can I help you?" asked a salesman.

"Uh, I'm just looking," Beth said, blushing. "Can I try out your display models?"

He flicked his hand in their direction and walked away.

"You're on, Tristan," Lacey said.

It didn't take Beth long to find the word-processing program. Tristan had to struggle to keep up with her, to think what her next thought might be, which was the way Lacey had taught him to slip into the minds of others.

When a writer looked at an empty computer screen, what did she see? Tristan wondered. A movie screen ready to be lit with faces? A night sky with one small star blinking at the top, a universe ready to be written on? Endless possibilities. Love's endless twists and turns—and all love's impossibilities.

Beth started typing:

Impossibilities

What did she see when she looked out every night at the lonely black screen of sky? Possibilities. Love's endless twists and turns, and, oh, bitter heart, all love's impossibilities.

Phew! Tristan thought.

"Phew!" Beth typed, then squinted at the screen.

"Stay with her, Tristan," Lacey said. "Keep your focus."

Back up. Delete word. Oh, bitter heart, Tristan prompted Beth.

"Oh, bitter heart, lonely heart," Beth typed, then paused.

They were both stuck, then Tristan saw the connection: You should not stay home alone.

"You should not stay home alone," Beth typed.

It's not safe alone, he thought.

"It's not safe alone," she typed.

Then, before he could send her a message about anything else, she wrote on: "But is my heart safe alone *with him?*"

No, he thought.

"Yes," Beth replied.

No!

"Yes!"

No!

"Yes!" Beth frowned.

Tristan sighed. Of course, she wanted the romance to work out and have the girl who was gazing at the night sky not be lonely anymore. But Tristan wanted to issue a warning. If Ivy was alone with the wrong guy . . .

"What's wrong?" asked Ivy.

"I've got that funny feeling again," Beth said. "It's really strange, like there's someone inside my head, saying things."

"Oh, you writers." Suzanne snorted.

Ivy bent down to look at the screen. "'No! Yes! No! Yes!'" she read, then laughed a little sadly. "It sounds like me when I first met Tristan."

"It's Tristan," Beth typed quickly.

Ivy stopped smiling.

Tristan pressed on, and Beth typed as fast as he thought: "Be careful, Ivy. It's dangerous, Ivy. Don't stay alone. Love you. Tristan."

Ivy straightened up. "That's not funny, Beth! That's stupid, and mean!"

Beth stared at the screen, her mouth open in disbelief.

Suzanne leaned down to read it. "Beth!" she said. "How could you? Ivy, wait!"

But Ivy was already halfway out of the store. Suzanne ran after her. Beth stared at the screen, her entire body shaking. Tristan slipped out of Beth's mind, exhausted.

"Would you like to print that out now?" the salesman asked, walking toward her.

Beth shook her head slowly and keyed in Delete Page. "Not this time," she said with tears in her eyes.

Every effort Tristan made to reach Ivy that week failed. What was worse, his attempts at warning her had pushed her further away from him and from those who cared for her. She was avoiding Beth, and now Philip too, after the little boy told her his angel said she must not stay alone. Tristan could have tried once more through Will, but he knew Ivy would just build another wall, a higher one.

Thursday night he headed for Riverstone Rise Cemetery, planning to get some rest, hoping to stave off the dreamless darkness so that he could keep watch over Ivy through the long weekend. On the way to his own grave, Tristan decided to go by Caroline's plot and see if fresh roses had been left there. He thought that Lacey was right: they had to find out who Caroline's visitor was and what he knew about her death.

Tristan crept along the cemetery road as if he were still flesh and blood, afraid of rousing the peaceful dead. In the moonlight, the white stones made a stark cityscape: obelisks towering like skyscrapers, mausoleums standing as mansions, the low rounded stones and shiny rectangular blocks marking neighborhoods of ordinary people. It was a still and eerie city, the city of the dead—my city, he thought grimly. Then he recognized the stone that marked one corner of the Baines family plot.

It was a well-kept plot with some ornate statuary, figures that seemed to watch Tristan as he approached Caroline's grave from behind. When he walked past her marker, he spun around with surprise. Sitting on Caroline's grass, lying back against her stone as if he were lounging in bed, was Eric. His arms and legs were limp, and his head was turned sideways, his cheek flat against the stone. For a moment Tristan wasn't sure if Eric was breathing. Moving closer, he saw that Eric's pale eyes were open, his pupils so dilated they looked as if he had drunk up two pools of night.

He was breathing softly, and he was mumbling something—something that made sense only to a mind high on drugs. Tristan wondered if Eric was capable of certain actions in this state. Could he stand up, could he walk? With his mind messed up like this, could he do something he'd wish later on that he hadn't done? Materializing his fingers, Tristan ran them across Eric's upturned palm.

Eric grabbed Tristan's fingers and for a moment

Tristan was caught. Then he let his fingers dissolve and pulled himself free.

"Been a while," Eric said, flexing the hand that had grabbed hold of Tristan. "Been too long, Caroline, sorry about that. A lot's been going on, a lot more than anybody knows." He laughed quietly and pointed, as if he could see her directly in front of him. "Of course, you know."

"I don't know," Tristan replied. "What's going on? Tell me."

Eric cocked his head, and for a moment Tristan thought he had heard the question.

"Yeah . . . probably," Eric said, answering some other question. "But it could be, you know, messy. I don't like things . . . messy."

Messy? Tristan wondered. What did that mean? Complicated? Bloody?

Eric sat straight up now, blinking his eyes, attentive to the voice he was hearing in his head. His hair was almost white in the moonlight, and his shadowed eyes stared holes through Tristan.

"You mean Ivy. Her name's Ivy," Eric said, waving his bony hand in the air. It passed directly through Tristan, chilling him like the touch of a skeleton.

"Well, what can I do?" Eric said. "You know where I'm at, Caroline. Don't push me! Back off!" He jumped to his feet and stood there, teetering.

81

Then he started to laugh low in his throat. "Yeah, yeah," he said. "This weekend everyone's going to the lake but Ivy." Eric smiled as if he'd just heard something funny. "Now, that's not a very nice thing to say!"

What, in his drug-crazed mind, did he think Caroline had said?

"Hey!" Eric shouted. "I *said* don't push me." He took two steps sideways. "Back off, Caroline. I don't want to listen to you anymore. *Back off!*"

Eric started running then, stumbling into markers and lurching from side to side, shrieking in a weird, high-pitched voice, "Back off, Caroline! Back off! Back off!"

Tristan watched him until he disappeared down the road. He tried to imagine the other half of Eric's conversation. What did Eric think Caroline wanted him to do?

Terrifying thoughts flooded Tristan's mind. Then he calmed himself and, focusing all his energy, called out, "Caroline, are you there?" He called her three times, hoping each time that she'd answer back. But his angel senses had already told him what the silence proved: There was nothing there but a cold body, and its answers were rotting with it.

6

Friday morning Gregory waved a piece of paper with a phone number on it at Ivy. "Promise me," he said.

She shrugged, then nodded halfheartedly.

"Juniper Lake is an hour and a half away, and the way I drive, just an hour," he added with a grin. "Promise me, Ivy."

"I can take care of myself," she told him, and rearranged the food in the ice chest for the fourth time. Maggie was feeding Andrew, Gregory, Philip, and herself that weekend but had packed enough additional food for a family of bears.

"I know you can take care of yourself," Gregory said, "but you still might get down or freaked out. This place can be pretty scary when you're alone." He rattled the paper. "If you need me—I don't care if it's in the middle of the night—call me."

Ivy gave a little duck of her head, which didn't mean that she would or wouldn't, then started packing the variety of cookies and chips that her mother had set out on the kitchen counter. "I hope you're ready to eat twenty-four hours a day," she told Gregory.

He laughed and opened one of the bags she was holding, snagging two cookies. He held one up to her mouth, and she bit it.

"I told you, Ivy, I won't squeal about you being alone here," Gregory said, "but the deal is that you have to call me once each day." He held her with his eyes. "Okay?"

She nodded.

"Promise," he said, his face close to hers. He held her with one finger hooked through her belt loop. "Promise."

"Okay, okay, I promise," she said, laughing.

He let her go. For a moment she wished that Gregory would stay home.

"I know what you're really up to," he teased. "As soon as we clear out of here, you'll be calling up people from all over and throwing a big bash."

"That's it," said Ivy, tossing a pack of napkins on top of the snack bag. "You've got me figured out."

"Have you thought about calling Will?" Gregory was still smiling, but his suggestion was serious.

"No," she said firmly.

"Why don't you like him?" he asked. "Not because of those angel drawings—"

"No, it's not that." Ivy checked the packs of paper plates and cups. They were from 'Tis the Season and decorated with Thanksgiving turkeys and Valentine hearts. "I like him all right. He just makes me uncomfortable. I can't quite explain it. When I look at him, there's something in his eyes. . . ."

Gregory laughed out loud. "Love? Or is it just raging hormones?"

"Right, right," Ivy said. "That must be it."

"I think so." He put his hands on her shoulders and would not let her turn away. "One of these days you'll realize that there are guys you don't even suspect who are looking at you . . . with something in their eyes."

Ivy looked down at her feet.

He laughed again and dropped his hands. "Be nice to Will," he said. "He's had some rough times in the past."

Before Ivy could ask what kind of rough times, Maggie and Philip came into the kitchen. Philip was wearing the Yankees cap and T-shirt that Gregory had bought him at the game.

Little by little, Philip was warming up to Gregory, and Gregory seemed pleased by it. Philip's talk of angels still annoyed him, but that was probably because it upset Ivy.

Philip gave Ivy a light punch in the arm. She had noticed lately that when others were around, her little brother wouldn't hug her. Maggie, who was dressed for the great outdoors from the neck down and made up for a photo session from the neck up, gave Ivy a squeeze and a kiss.

Gregory and Philip immediately rubbed their faces in the same place. Ivy grinned at them but left the fresh, red print of lips on her cheek.

"That's my girl," Maggie said. "Got us all packed up. I swear, I raised you to be a better mother than me."

Ivy laughed.

Gregory carried out the ice chest, and the others followed with bags and suitcases, putting them in Maggie's car. Gregory planned to take his own car, and Andrew, who had been held up by a late-afternoon meeting, would drive up to the lake afterward.

There was a lot of car door banging and loud spurts of music. Philip, who wanted to ride with Gregory, was fooling around with his stereo. At last both cars drove off, and Ivy stood alone, cherishing the silence. The afternoon was warm and still, and only the trees, the very tops of them, rustled dryly. It was one of the few moments of real peace that she had felt since Tristan's death.

She went inside and grabbed a book, one that Beth had given her, so it was sure to be a torrid romance. Beth had sent it via Suzanne with a note of apology, afraid to face Ivy and afraid to call her up. Ivy had telephoned Beth to let her know she wasn't angry anymore.

She was still mystified, however. It was such an odd thing for Beth to have done—creating computer messages from "Tristan." Beth was usually so sensitive to other people's feelings. Well, she had thought that Will was sensitive, too, and look what he had done: put a pair of wings on Tristan.

In spite of the pain of that memory, Ivy smiled a little. What would Tristan have thought about Will turning him into an angel?

She read for more than an hour and a half up in the tree house, occasionally gazing out through the branches at the distant glittering strip that was the river. Then she stuck the book in the waistband of her jeans and swung down on the rope. In the mood for a walk, Ivy circled around the front of the house and headed down the winding drive. She quickened her pace, and kept it up as she climbed the hill again, returning to the top, sweaty and exhilarated.

Maybe she could finally play "Liebestraum," she thought. With all this quiet around her, maybe she'd play up a storm, and work all the way through the love song. She had been practicing for the festival every day but hadn't been able to get to the end of the piece. At some point the memories always came back to her, a slow tide turning in her, and washed out all her music. Maybe that day she could hold on to the notes.

Ivy grabbed a soda from the kitchen and hurried upstairs to take a shower. Halfway through it, she wondered if she should have locked the back door. Don't be silly, she told herself. No one ever comes up on this hill. She intended to enjoy these days of peace and wouldn't let the worrying of Suzanne, Beth, and Gregory put her on edge.

When Ivy climbed the steps to her music room, Ella scooted ahead of her and leaped up onto the piano bench.

Ivy smiled. "You're practicing for the festival, too?"

She thought about the triplets of notes that Ella had "played" the week before, then pushed it out of her mind; the song would make her start thinking of Tristan.

Ivy began her warm-ups, then played melodies that were Philip's favorites, and finally began "Liebestraum." She was pleased by her playing, her fingers flying over the keys, caught up completely in the vibrant cadenza. Just before she returned to the opening theme, in the moment she paused to turn the page, she heard a noise.

Immediately she thought of glass shattering. Her flesh turned to goose bumps, but she fought against her fear. She reminded herself that breaking glass was a sound from her nightmares. If anyone really wanted to get in, all the person had to do was open the back door. The noise wasn't a window breaking, she told herself. A tree branch fell against the house, or something had blown over downstairs.

Still, Ivy felt uneasy. She glanced around the room and saw that Ella was gone. Maybe the cat had knocked over something. The best thing to do would be to investigate and prove to herself that it was nothing. Ivy went to the top of the attic stairs and listened.

She thought the noise had come from the west wing, by Andrew's office. Maybe it was Andrew, out of his meeting early, stopping by the house to pick up something.

Ivy crept down the steps to her bedroom and stopped just inside the door that led to the hall. She wished Ella were with her; the cat could warn her with a prick of her ears or a twitch of her tail.

The house seemed suddenly huge, twice its real size, pocked with a hundred hiding places and far away from anyone who could hear her scream. Ivy stepped back and picked up the telephone in her room, then put it down.

Get ahold of yourself, she thought. You can't drag the police all the way out here for nothing.

"Andrew?" she called. "Andrew, is that you?"

No answer.

"Ella, come here. Where are you, Ella?"

The house was deafeningly silent.

Ivy tiptoed into the hall and decided to go down the center stairway rather than the narrower one that led into the west wing. There was a phone on the table in the lower hall. If she noticed that anything had been disturbed, she'd immediately make a call from there.

At the bottom of the stairs Ivy looked quickly left and right. Maybe she should just run out the front door, she thought.

And then what? Let someone take what he wanted? Or better yet, let him find a snug spot to lie in wait for her?

Don't let your imagination run away with you, she chided herself.

The rooms on the east side of the house—the living room, library, and solarium—were closed up, still shuttered against the early sunlight. Ivy turned the other way, peeking around the corner into the dining room. She walked through it, tensing at the creak of old boards, and pushed open the door to the kitchen. Across from her was the door she had left unlocked, still closed. After quickly checking two closets, she locked the outside door.

But what about the basement? She bolted the door on the kitchen side. She could check the outside entrance to it later, she thought, then headed into the family room. Nothing had been disturbed.

Just as she stepped into the gallery that led to Andrew's office, Ella came trotting toward her.

"Ella!" Ivy breathed out with relief. "What have you been up to?"

Ella swished her tail fiercely back and forth.

"First it was his chair," Ivy said, shaking her finger at the cat, though she was gasping with relief. "Now what, a Waterford vase?"

She marched into the room and stopped.

A windowpane was smashed in, the door next to it ajar. Ivy stepped back.

She stepped into him. "Wha—?"

Before she could turn around, a sack was pulled over her head. Ivy screamed and fought to get free, ripping at the sack with her hands, clawing it like a cat. The more she yanked at the cloth, the tighter it was pulled around her. She felt as if she were suffocating.

She fought to keep herself from panicking, struggling against someone much stronger than she. Think! Think! she told herself.

Her feet were still free. But she knew that if she kicked and lost her balance, he'd have her. She began to use her weight, swinging her whole body from side to side. She swung hard. He lost his grip, and Ivy spun away.

Then he grabbed her again. He was pushing her now, toward a wall or a corner, she thought. She couldn't see a thing inside the dark bag and had lost track of where she was. Even if she could get free of him, she didn't know which way to run.

The sack was so rough that each time he pulled it the threads burned against her face. She wanted to lift her hands and claw her way through so she could see her attacker's face.

He made no sound. She felt him shift his grip, holding her now with just one arm. Then she felt it, something pressed against her head, something hard and round—like the barrel of a gun.

She began to kick and kick, and shriek.

Then she heard a pounding sound from somewhere else in the house. Someone was pounding and calling, "Ivy! Ivy!"

She tried to answer.

She was hurtled forward and could not stop herself from falling. She slammed against something as hard as rock and slid down it. Metal things tumbled and clattered around her. Then everything went black.

*   *   *

"Ivy! Ivy!" Tristan called.

"Ivy! Ivy!" Will shouted, pounding on the front door. Then he raced around the outside of the house, looking for some other way in.

He saw Gregory's car parked in the back. He stopped—Tristan stopped—at the broken window and the door that opened into Andrew's office.

"Ivy, what the— Who did this?" Gregory was saying, bending over her, gently pulling off the sack. "Are you okay? Easy now. You're safe now."

Fireplace tools were scattered on the floor. Ivy rubbed her head and stared up at Gregory. Then they both turned to look at Will, who was framed by the open door. Tristan had just slipped out of Will, but he saw the fear and mistrust in Ivy's face and the angry flush on Gregory's.

"What are you doing here?" Gregory demanded.

Will was speechless, and even if Tristan had stayed inside him, he couldn't have given an answer that would have satisfied Gregory or Ivy.

"I don't know," Will said. "I just thought— I just knew I had to be here. I felt something was wrong and that I had to come."

With the angry color draining out of Gregory's face, his skin looked paler than normal. He looked almost as shaken as Ivy.

"Are you all right, Ivy?" Will asked.

She nodded and turned away, resting her head against Gregory's chest.

"Is there anything I can do?" Will asked.

"No."

"I'd better call the police," he said.

"You'd better," Gregory said, his voice cold and unfriendly.

When Will placed the call, he spoke calmly, but Tristan knew that his partner was as shaken and bewildered as he. Tristan knew little more than Will about how he had first sensed that Ivy was in danger.

She needs you. The message had come to Tristan, though whether he'd heard it or simply understood it, he couldn't say. But knowing that something was about to happen, and remembering that Lacey had said he could not rescue her himself, that he had to combine his powers with someone else's, he had rushed right to Will, urging him to go to Ivy, to help her.

It had been a struggle, especially at the beginning. Tristan had to learn to channel his energy, and gradually Will gave himself over to his direction. Tristan wondered if Will realized he had driven up the hill at eighty miles per hour, despite the upgrade and turns. Did Will remember racing around from the front to the back of the house faster than was humanly possible?

But still not fast enough to catch Ivy's attacker, thought Tristan. Until he knew who the attacker was, there was no way of guessing when he'd strike next, or how Will and he could protect Ivy.

Will and he. He and Will. There was no denying now that Will cared for Ivy—and that Tristan needed him to.

Tristan watched as Gregory picked up Ivy and carried her to the sofa. Ella crouched under Andrew's desk, her eyes glowing like embers.

"Who was it, Ella?" Tristan asked. "You're the only one who saw it. Who did this?"

Will left the room and came back with an icepack.

Gregory held it gently against Ivy's head. "I'm here. Everything's going to be all right," he said over and over, continually rubbing her back and soothing her.

Before long they heard the whine of a siren. A police car swung into the driveway, followed unexpectedly by another car. Andrew's.

"What happened?" Andrew cried, rushing into the house with the officers. "Ivy, are you all right?"

He looked at the broken window, then at Will, and finally turned his attention to Gregory. "Why are you here?" he asked. "You're supposed to be with Maggie and Philip."

"Why are *you?*" Gregory asked back.

Andrew glanced quickly at the police, then gestured toward his desk. "I left some papers behind, some reports I wanted to work on at the lake."

"I came because Ivy called me," Gregory said. "I'd told her earlier today that she should call me if she needed anything." He gazed down at her. Ivy met his eyes with a puzzled expression.

"It was you who called me, wasn't it?" he asked.

"No."

Gregory looked surprised, then squeezed her hands hard and dropped them. "Whew," he said softly. "You owe somebody big time."

He turned to the others. "When we got to the lake, I had to run out to the store. Maggie had remembered everything for our trip, except toilet paper.

"When I returned, the man at the lodge said someone had called three times, asking for me, but didn't leave a message. I figured it was Ivy. It's been rough for her lately—you know that," he said, appealing to his father. "I didn't waste any time. I came right home."

"Lucky girl," remarked one of the police officers.

The police began to ask questions then. Tristan moved slowly around the room, studying faces and reading what the police were scribbling down.

Was it jealousy that he felt every time he saw Gregory touch Ivy? Or was it some kind of intuition? he wondered. Was Ivy really safe in Gregory's arms?

Had Gregory told Eric that Ivy would be alone all weekend? If Eric was responsible for this, would Gregory cover for him?

And why had Gregory questioned his father? Did he think Andrew's excuse for returning to the house was a little too convenient?

The police stayed a long time that afternoon and asked lots of questions, but it seemed to Tristan they were all the wrong ones.

7

When Ivy answered the door on Tuesday morning, she knew that Beth had read the local paper. Her friend stepped inside with a quick, shy "How're you doing?" She hugged Ivy, nearly squeezing the breath out of her, then backed off, blushing.

"I'm fine," said Ivy. "I'm really fine."

"Are you?" Beth looked like a worried mother owl, her eyes wide, her frosted hair falling out of its knot in soft feathers. She stared at Ivy's bruised cheek.

"It's the newest thing since tattoos," Ivy said, smiling and touching her face lightly.

"Your face looks like . . . a pansy."

Ivy laughed. "Purple and yellow. I'm going to look great for the festival. You got anything that matches?"

Beth tried to smile, but ended up biting her lip.

"Come on back," Ivy said, leading her to the kitchen. "Let's get something to drink. We have to stick around here for a few minutes. I'm getting interviewed for the third time."

"By a newspaper?"

"By the police."

"The police! Ivy, did you tell them—" Beth hesitated.

"Tell them what?"

"About the computer messages," Beth said quietly.

"No." Ivy pulled out a bar stool for Beth to sit on. "Why should I? It was nothing more than a strange coincidence. You were just fooling around and—"

The look in Beth's eyes stopped her. "I wasn't fooling around."

Ivy shrugged a little, then measured out some coffee beans. Since Friday evening she had been acting as if nothing much had happened, as if she had already gotten over the scare. She felt bad about ruining everyone's weekend and tried to keep them from worrying and fussing over her. But the truth was, she was glad to have her family home with her. She was starting to get spooked.

Philip was convinced an angel had sent

Gregory to save her—the same angel who had prevented him from tumbling out of the tree house, he said. Recently he had found a statue of an angelic baseball player and claimed it had been delivered to him by a glowing friend of his own guardian.

Ivy knew her brother was talking like this because he was frightened. Maybe, Ivy thought, having lost Tristan, Philip was scared of losing her, too. Maybe that was why he had warned her several times about the train climbing up the ridge to get her.

How could she blame him? With the car accident, then Friday's close call, Ivy herself imagined hidden dangers wherever she looked. And if there was one thing she didn't need just then, it was Beth looking at her as if she had glimpsed something frightening from beyond.

"Beth, you're my friend, and you were worried about me being alone, the same way Suzanne and Gregory were worried. The difference is, you're a writer and—and you've got a very active imagination," Ivy added, smiling. "It's only natural that when you worry, it comes out in a story."

Beth didn't look convinced.

"In any case, you're not responsible. Even if you were psychic, psychics only know about things, they don't make them happen."

The doorbell rang, and Ivy quickly dried her hands. "So there's no reason to tell the police."

"Tell them what?" Gregory asked, coming into the kitchen.

He was up earlier than usual, dressed for a day in New York City with Suzanne.

"Tell Gregory about it, Beth, if it would make you feel any better," Ivy advised, then went to answer the door.

A redheaded man sucking on a breath mint was pacing the front porch as if he had been waiting for hours. He identified himself as Lieutenant Donnelly and asked Ivy if he could speak with her in the office where the assault had occurred.

"I'll see," Ivy replied. "My stepfather didn't go to the college today, and if he's working—"

"Is he in? Good," the detective said briskly. "He's on my list, too."

A few minutes later they were joined in Andrew's office by Gregory. The detective had questions for all of them, but most of what they talked about were facts they had gone over before.

When they were finished, the lieutenant said, "Our reason for questioning you again is that we had a similar incident late last night in Ridgefield. Same style of break-in, victim a high-school girl, got a bag pulled over her head. If our friend is embarking on a series of such attacks, we want to find as many similarities as possible. That way we can establish a pattern, predict him—and nail him."

"Then you've concluded that the attack on Ivy was a random act," Andrew said, "rather than something done by someone who knows her?"

"We haven't concluded anything," the detective replied, leaning forward, raising his bushy red eyebrows, "and I'm always interested in other people's theories."

"I have no theories," Andrew said crisply. "I just want to know if she is safe now."

"Is there some reason you think she isn't? Is there anyone you know who would want to hurt a member of your family?"

"No," Andrew replied. Then he turned to Gregory. "Not that I can think of," he said slowly. "Do you know of anyone, Gregory?"

Gregory let the question hang in the air for a moment. "Nope."

Andrew turned back to the detective. "We just want to know if we can assume that Ivy is safe."

"Of course. I understand, sir," Donnelly said. "And of course you understand that I can't assure you of that." He handed Ivy his card. "If you remember anything else, give me a call."

"About the girl in Ridgefield," Ivy said, catching the detective's sleeve. "Is she okay?"

The man's mouth formed a grim line. He shook his head twice. "Dead," he said quietly, then pushed open the door next to the newly fixed windowpane. "I can let myself out."

As soon as he'd left, Ivy hurried out of the room, not wanting the others to see her tears. Gregory caught her halfway up the back stairs. She scrambled away from him and went down on all fours. He pulled her to him.

"Ivy. Talk to me. What is it?"

She pulled away from him and pressed her lips together.

"What is it?"

"It could have happened to me!" she blurted. "If you hadn't come at that moment, if you hadn't scared him away—" Tears tumbled down her cheeks.

"It didn't happen," he said gently but firmly, and sat her down on the steps.

Don't leave now, Ivy begged silently. Don't go out with Suzanne today. I need you more than she does.

Immediately she felt guilty about those thoughts.

Gregory wiped away her tears.

"Sorry," Ivy said.

"Sorry for what?"

"For acting so—so—"

"Human?"

She rested against him.

He brushed the hair back from her face and let his fingers stay tangled in it.

"My father was right, you know. For once, old Andrew got it right. I feel sorry for the other girl's family, but I'm pretty relieved. Now we know it wasn't someone out to get you." He pulled his head back to look at her. "And that lets Will off the hook," he joked.

Ivy didn't laugh.

"Unless Will has a career we don't know about. He can be awfully silent and mysterious. . . ."

Ivy still didn't smile. She breathed as evenly as possible, trying to stifle her hiccoughs. "You'd better get going, Gregory," she advised. "Do you realize what time it is? Suzanne doesn't like her dates to be late."

"I know," he said, and held Ivy apart from him, studying her.

Does he look at Suzanne that way, she wondered, so intently, as if he's searching out her thoughts? Does he look into her eyes the way he looks into mine? Does he care about her as much as he cares about me?

Another wave of guilt washed over Ivy; her face must have revealed it.

"What?" he asked. "What are you thinking?"

"Nothing. You'd better get going."

He continued to look at her uncertainly.

"On your way out, would you stop and tell Beth I'll be down in a minute?"

He shrugged, then let go of her. "Sure."

Ivy hurried up the steps. She was glad she'd be spending most of her day off with Beth. If Ivy told her she didn't want to talk about something, Beth would drop the subject. Unfortunately, she had already agreed to meet Suzanne for dinner that evening, after Gregory and she returned from New York. Ivy wasn't looking forward to hashing over the details of Gregory's heroic rescue and every "he said, I said" of Suzanne's date.

Ivy had just passed Gregory's room when his phone rang. She wondered if she should pick it up for him or let the answering machine take a message.

It's probably Suzanne, Ivy thought, calling to find out where he is. She stopped to listen; if it was her friend, she'd pick up the phone and tell her that Gregory was on his way.

The machine beeped. There was a moment of silence, then a voice said, "It's me. I need the money, Gregory. You know I don't like to go to your old man. And you know what will happen if I don't get the money. I need the money, Gregory, now."

The caller hung up without identifying himself, but she recognized his voice. Eric.

*   *   *

Ivy drummed her fingers on the wicker chair, looked out at the pond behind the Goldsteins' house, and checked her watch once more. Obviously Suzanne had forgotten about their plans. They were to meet there at six-thirty. It was now twenty-five minutes past seven.

Ivy was annoyed that she had waited this long, especially since she didn't even want to see Suzanne that night. But she thought that as a loyal best friend she should stick it out.

"Always your best friend," she murmured. At home she had a large box of tattered letters, notes that Suzanne had started writing in fourth grade whenever she got bored in class. All the letters were signed, "Always your best friend."

Always—but the truth was, with Gregory around, things were changing between the two of them. And Suzanne was as guilty as she. Ivy got up from the chair abruptly and started down the porch steps.

From the other side of the house came the sound of a car in the driveway. A door slammed. Ivy circled around the house, then stopped. Gregory and Suzanne were walking slowly toward the house, their arms around each other, Suzanne's head on his shoulder. Ivy wished she had left earlier, much earlier.

Gregory spotted her first and stopped walking.

Then Suzanne looked up. "Hi, Ivy!" she said with surprise. A moment later, her hand flew up to her head. "Oh, no, I totally forgot! I'm so sorry. I hope you haven't been waiting too long."

Since six-thirty, and you know it, and I'm starved, Ivy wanted to say, but didn't. But she also didn't play Suzanne's game by reassuring her in some way: No, no, I just got here myself. That's what she was supposed to say, wasn't it? Ivy just looked at her friend and let her figure it out.

Perhaps Gregory picked up on some of the tension between them. He jumped in quickly. "We decided at the last minute to get a pizza at Celentano's. I'm sorry we didn't know you were here, Ivy. It would have been great if you'd come with us."

He was rewarded with two glares: Suzanne's, for implying that dinner would have been great if Ivy had come; Ivy's, for suggesting that she'd enjoy being with them on a date. Hadn't he ever heard that three's a crowd?

Gregory unwrapped himself from Suzanne, then retreated toward the car. Slipping one hand in his pocket, he propped the other on the open door, trying to look casual.

"I can see there's going to be some talking here tonight, some dirt-dishing. Maybe I should leave before I get hooked by the soap opera."

You *are* the soap opera, Ivy thought.

"You may as well," Suzanne replied. "Most guys are amateurs at talking."

Gregory laughed—not as much at ease as he pretended, Ivy thought—then rattled his keys at them and left.

"I'm beat," Suzanne said, throwing herself down on the front steps and pulling Ivy down next to her. "Manhattan in the summer—I tell you, it brings out the crazies. You should have seen all the people at Times Square, waiting for another vision of—"

She stopped herself, but Ivy knew what she was about to say. She had already read about the angelic Barbra Streisand.

Suzanne reached out then and touched Ivy's face very, very gently. "Aren't they getting tired of seeing you in the emergency room?"

Ivy laughed a little.

"How're you feeling?" Suzanne asked.

"All right . . . really," she added when she saw the doubt in Suzanne's eyes.

"Are you dreaming about this now, too?"

"I haven't so far," said Ivy.

"You're tough, girl," Suzanne said, shaking her head. "And I bet you're hungry and ready to kill me."

"Very hungry and almost ready," Ivy replied as Suzanne pushed herself up from the steps and dug in her purse for her house keys. Peppermint, Suzanne's Pomeranian, greeted them with yaps of joy, anticipating dinner. They headed straight for the kitchen.

While Suzanne fed Peppermint, Ivy explored the Goldstein's refrigerator, which was always well stocked. She settled for a large bowl of homemade soup. Suzanne set a pan of brownies and some lemon frosted cupcakes on the table between them. She cut herself a brownie, then swiveled back and forth in her chair. "I've got him, Ivy," she said. "Gregory's definitely hooked. Now all I have to do is reel him in."

"I thought you were going to reel him in last week, or maybe the week before," Ivy recalled.

"That's why I need your help," Suzanne said quickly. "I'm never sure with Gregory. I have to know, Ivy—did he go out with any girls this weekend? I mean, with me being away and him having to come home because of you, I wondered whether he got out his little date book and . . ."

Ivy chased noodles around with her soup spoon. "I don't know," she said.

"How can you not know? You live with him!"

"He was home Saturday morning. In the afternoon we played tennis and went shopping. At night he went to a movie with Philip and me. He was out for a while on Sunday afternoon, but the rest of the time he was with Philip and me."

"*And you.* It's a good thing you're my best friend and Gregory's stepsister," Suzanne remarked, "or else I'd be insanely jealous and suspicious. Lucky for both of us, isn't it?"

"Yeah," Ivy replied without enthusiasm.

"How about Monday? Did he go out then?"

"For a while in the morning, then late last night. Suzanne, I don't feel right reporting on him to you."

"Well, whose side are you on?" her friend asked.

Ivy crumbled a cracker in her soup. "I didn't know there were sides."

"Who do you feel most loyal to, me or Gregory?" Suzanne persisted. "You know, in the beginning I thought you didn't like him. In fact, I thought you couldn't stand him but didn't say anything because you didn't want to hurt my feelings."

Ivy nodded. "I didn't know him very well then. But I do now, and since I care about him and I care about you, and since you're chasing him—"

"I've caught him, Ivy."

"Since you've caught him, and you hooked *me* years ago, how can there be sides?"

"Don't be so naive," Suzanne replied. "There are always sides in love." She chopped away at the brownies in the pan. "Love is war."

"Don't, Suzanne."

She stopped chopping. "Don't what?"

"Don't do what you're doing to him."

Suzanne sat back in her chair. "Just what are you saying?" There was a noticeable chill in her voice.

"I'm saying don't play games with him. Don't push him around the way you've pushed around the other guys. He deserves better treatment, much better."

Suzanne was silent for a moment. "You know what you need, Ivy? A boyfriend of your own."

Ivy stared down at her soup.

"And Gregory agrees with me on that."

Ivy glanced up sharply.

"He thinks Will is perfect for you."

"Tristan was perfect for me."

"Was," said Suzanne. *"Was.* Life goes on, and you've got to go on with it!"

"I will when I'm ready," Ivy replied.

"You've got to let go of the past." Suzanne laid her hand on Ivy's wrist. "You've got to stop acting like a little girl, holding on to the hand of big brother Gregory."

Ivy looked away.

"You've got to start getting out and seeing other guys. Will's a start."

"Butt out, Suzanne."

"Gregory and I can set you up."

"I said, butt out!"

"All right!"

Suzanne sliced an ultrathin piece of brownie, then pointed the knife at Ivy. "But you butt out, too, and don't tell me what to do. I'm warning you now, don't interfere with me and Gregory."

What did she mean by interfere? Ivy wondered. Don't give her advice—or stop holding on to Gregory's hand?

They both stared down at their food in silence. Peppermint sat between their chairs, looking from one to the other. Then somehow, after what seemed an interminable silence, they found their way onto safer ground, talking about the wedding Suzanne had been to. But as Suzanne talked on and Ivy nodded, all Ivy could think of was that one way or the other, she was going to lose someone who meant a lot to her.

8

"Give us a few more minutes, Philip," Ivy said. "We want to look at the rest of these paintings."

"I think I'll go find Gregory."

Ivy reached out quickly and caught her brother by the back of his T-shirt. "Not today. You're stuck with Beth and me."

For the last four days Ivy had spent little time with Gregory, seeing him only at occasional family meals and in chance passings in the hall. Whenever their paths did cross, she'd been careful not to start a long conversation with him. When he'd sought her out—and the more she'd avoided him the more he had sought her out—she'd claimed she was on her way up to the music room to practice.

Gregory looked puzzled and a little angry about the distance she was putting between them. But what else could she do? They had grown too close. Without meaning to, Ivy had come to depend on him. If she didn't back off now, she might lose Suzanne as a friend.

Suzanne and Beth had met Gregory, Philip, and Ivy in town that afternoon, at the bottom of Main Street, where the festival began. Suzanne had immediately draped her arm across Gregory's back and slipped her hand into his back pocket, walking him away from Ivy and Philip. Ivy had responded by steering Philip in another direction. Beth was left standing on the street corner.

"Come with us," Ivy had called to her. "We're going to see the art."

The display was set up along a narrow lane of old shops that ran back from Main Street. An assortment of townspeople—women pushing baby strollers, old ladies in straw hats, kids with their faces painted, and two guys dressed as clowns—walked along looking at the pictures, trying to guess who the artists were. Each picture was titled and numbered, but the artists' names were masked for the judging that would take place later that day.

Ivy, Beth, and Philip were almost at the end of the display when Philip had started fussing about finding Gregory.

Now Ivy pointed to a strange painting, trying

to distract him. "What do you think that is?" she asked.

"Things." He read the title with a scowl.

"Looks to me like a row of lipsticks," Beth said, "or trees in the fall or Christmas candles or catsup bottles or missiles at sunset—"

Philip screwed up his face. "It looks to me like it's stupid," he said loudly.

"Shh! Philip, keep your voice down," Ivy warned. "For all we know, the artist is right behind us."

Philip turned around to look. Suddenly the scowl was gone. His face lit up. "No," he said, "but there's an—" He hesitated.

"What?" Beth asked.

Ivy glanced quickly behind her. No one was there.

Philip gave a little shrug. "Never mind." He sighed.

They moved on to the last entry, a panel with four watercolors.

"Wow!" Beth said. "These are fabulous! Number thirty-three, whoever you are, you're my winner."

"Mine, too," Ivy agreed. The artist's colors were almost transparent and infused with a light of their own.

Ivy pointed to a painting of a garden. "I wish I could sit there, for hours and hours. It makes me feel so peaceful."

"I like the snake," Philip observed.

Only a little boy would have found that snake, Ivy thought, painted in so slyly.

"I want to talk to the woman in the last picture," Beth said.

The woman sat under a tree with her face turned away from the painter. Blossoms were streaming down on her, luminous apple blossoms, but they made Ivy think of snow. She looked at the title: *Too Soon.*

"There's a story behind that one," Beth said softly.

Ivy nodded. She knew the story, or one like it, about losing someone before you had a chance to—

For a moment her eyes stung. Then she blinked and said, "Well, we've seen everything in the show. Let's go spend money."

"Yeah!" Philip shouted. "Where're the rides?"

"There aren't any rides, not at a festival like this."

Philip stopped short. "No rides?" He couldn't believe it. "No rides!"

"I think we're in for a long afternoon," Ivy told Beth.

"We'll just keep feeding him," Beth replied.

"I want to go home."

"Let's walk back to Main Street," Ivy suggested, "and see what everyone is selling."

"That's boring." Her brother was getting that

stiff-jawed look that meant trouble. "I'm going to find Gregory."

"No!" She said it so sharply that Beth glanced over at her.

"He's on a date, Philip," Ivy reminded him quietly, "and we can't bother him."

Philip started dragging his feet as though he had been walking for miles. Beth was walking slowly, too, studying Ivy.

"It's just that it's really not fair to Gregory," Ivy told Beth, as if she had asked for an explanation. "He's not used to a nine-year-old tagging along everywhere."

"Oh." The way Beth glanced away told Ivy that her friend knew this wasn't the whole truth.

"And of course, Suzanne's not used to it at all."

"I guess not," Beth replied mildly.

"This is boring, boring, boring," Philip complained. "I want to go home."

"Then walk!" Ivy snapped.

Beth glanced around. "How about getting our picture taken?" she suggested. "Every year there's a stand called Old West Photos. They have different costumes you can dress up in. It's fun."

"Great idea!" Ivy replied. "We'll take enough for an album," she added under her breath, "if it keeps him occupied."

The canopied stand was set up in front of the photo shop and looked like a small stage set.

119

There were several backdrops to choose from, trunks of clothes that kids and adults were sorting through, and props scattered about—pistols, wooden mugs, a fake-fur buffalo head. Tinkly piano music gave the tent a saloon atmosphere.

The photographer himself was dressed up in a cowboy hat, vest, and tight cowhide pants. Beth eyed him from behind. "Cute," she observed. "Very cute."

Ivy smiled.

"I like anything in boots," Beth said, a little too loudly.

The cowboy turned around.

"Will!"

Will laughed at Beth, who flushed with embarrassment. He put a reassuring hand on her arm, then nodded at Ivy. Philip had already strayed toward the costume trunks.

"How are you?" Will asked.

Beth banged herself on the head. "I completely forgot that with your job, you'd be doing this."

He smiled at her—a big and easy smile. It was impossible to see Will's eyes under the shadow of his hat, but Ivy could tell when he glanced from Beth to her, because the smile became not so big, and not so easy.

"Thinking about having your picture done?" he asked.

120

Philip was already elbow-deep in clothes.

"Looks like our date wants to," Beth said to Ivy.

"Your date?"

"My brother, Philip," Ivy explained. He had wedged himself in between two guys big enough to play pro football. "The short one."

Will nodded. "Maybe I should steer him toward another trunk. Ladies' costumes are over there," Will added over his shoulder, pointing toward trunks where a flock of girls were gathered.

A few of the girls were older than Ivy and Beth. Others looked two or three years younger. All of them kept turning around, looking at Will and giggling.

"Hey, cowboy," Beth called softly after him. "I bet *they'd* like your help, even more than Philip."

"They're doing fine," he said, and continued on.

"Love those buns."

Will stopped.

Ivy looked at Beth, and Beth looked at Ivy. Ivy knew she hadn't said it, but Beth acted as if she hadn't, either. Her blue eyes were brimming with laughter and surprise.

"I didn't say it."

"Neither did I."

Will just shook his head and walked on.

"But you were thinking it," someone said. Ivy glanced around.

"Well, maybe I was, Ivy," Beth admitted, "but—"

Will turned around.

"I didn't say it!" Ivy insisted.

"Say what?" Will asked, cocking his head.

Ivy was sure he had heard. "That you have— That I thought— That—" Ivy looked sideways at Beth. "Oh, never mind."

"What is she talking about?" Will asked Beth.

"Something about your buns," said Beth.

Ivy threw up her hands. "I don't care about his buns!"

The buzz of voices beneath the canopy ceased. Everyone looked at Will, then Ivy.

"Would you like to see mine?" asked one of the football types.

"Oh, jeez," Ivy said.

Will laughed out loud.

"Your cheeks are pink," Beth told Ivy.

Ivy put her hands up to her face.

Beth pulled them away. "It's a much better color for you than purple and yellow."

Fifteen minutes later, Ivy grimaced as Beth zipped her up in front of the dressing room mirror.

"If I lean over, Will's going to get a fine shot."

"He's going to get a fine shot even with you straightened up," Beth observed.

They had decided to dress as saloon girls in identical red-and-black dresses, "floozy frocks," as

Beth called them. She smoothed her hands over her ample hips. "I don't care if my man's law-abiding," she said with a Western twang, "so long as he abides by *my* laws."

Ivy laughed, then gave a backward glance at herself in the mirror. Beth had given her the smaller dress to wear; there wasn't a curve that didn't show. Ivy was reluctant to step through the dressing room curtains, though Beth informed her that the two football types had left. Ivy could deal with the Brothers Macho; it was Will she felt shy around.

Maybe he sensed that. He stretched out his hand to Beth, as she and Ivy stepped out of the dressing room. "Oh, Miss Lizzie," he said, "you do look mighty fine today. You too, Miss Ivy," he added quietly.

"How about me?" Philip asked. He came out in fringed pants and a vest that almost fit him. But the ten-gallon hat was about nine gallons too big.

"Fearsome," Will said. "Fearsome and awesome, if only I could see your chin."

Ivy laughed, feeling more comfortable again.

"How about if we try a different size?"

"Make it black," said Philip.

"Right, Slim."

Will found a hat and got the three of them lined up in front of the camera, angling them just right. Then he pushed his hat back and went behind the camera. It was a new camera in the body of an old one, rigged up to give off a big puff of smoke—that was part of the show. But after the flash and the smoke, Will's head shot up from behind the equipment. He looked almost comical, and at first Ivy thought that too was part of the show. But the way Will was staring made all three of them turn to look behind them.

"I—uh—I'm going to take another," he said. "Can you set yourselves just like before?"

They did, and a second puff of smoke was sent up.

"What went wrong the first time?" Beth asked.

"I'm not sure." A look Ivy couldn't interpret passed between him and Beth. He shook his head. Then the hat was back over his eyes again. "These will take a few minutes to print. Do you want two or three copies?" Will asked them.

"Two's fine," Ivy replied. "One for Beth and one for us."

"I want my own copy," said Philip.

"So do I," said another voice.

Everyone turned.

"Howdy, pardner," Gregory said, holding his hand out to Philip. "Ladies." His eyes lingered on Ivy, traveling down her slowly.

Suzanne gave her a quicker look. "You sure squeezed yourself into that one," she remarked. "It's a wonder a crowd hasn't gathered."

Will pulled on his tight pants. "Are you talking about her or me?" he asked lightly.

Gregory laughed. Beth laughed after Gregory did, then glanced uncomfortably at Suzanne. Suzanne wasn't amused.

Will shoved two film cartridges in the developing machine and set up for his next group of customers.

"Suzanne, there were only two dresses alike," Ivy said quickly, "and Beth and I wanted to match, so she took that one and I took— Tell her, Beth."

But as Beth repeated the explanation, Ivy said to herself, Why bother? Until Gregory learns to keep his eyes from wandering to other girls, it's hopeless. I wish he'd wander them over to Beth, though.

She turned toward the dressing room.

Gregory caught her by the arm. "We'll wait for you," he said. "We're going to check out Will's paintings."

Ivy saw Suzanne out of the corner of her eye, drumming her fingers on the top of a trunk, her pinky ring flashing.

"We've already seen them," Ivy told him.

"Though we didn't know which were his," Beth said. "The artists' names are still covered."

"They're watercolors," Gregory told them.

"Watercolors?" Ivy and Beth repeated at the same time.

"Will," Gregory called out. "What's your entry number?"

"Thirty-three," he replied.

Beth and Ivy exchanged glances.

"You painted the garden where Ivy wants to sit for hours," Beth said.

"And the snake," Philip said.

"And the woman with blossoms falling around her like snow," Ivy added.

"That's right." Will continued to work, arranging his customers before the camera.

"They were amazing!" Beth said.

"I like the snake," said Philip.

Ivy watched Will without saying anything. He was being the cool Will O'Leary again, acting as if his paintings and what they said about them didn't matter to him. Then she saw the quick turn of the head, as if he were checking to see whether she was still there. She realized then that he had wanted her to make a comment.

"Your paintings are really . . . uh . . ." All the words she could think of sounded flat.

"That's okay," he said, cutting her short before she could come up with the right description.

"Are you coming along for a second look?" Gregory asked impatiently.

"Be out in a minute," Beth replied, hurrying toward the dressing room.

Philip was walking to the dressing room and undressing at the same time.

"I can't," Ivy said to Gregory. "I play at five o'clock and I need to—"

"Practice?" His eyes flashed.

"I need time to collect myself, to think through what I'm playing, that's all. I can't do that with everyone around."

"I'm sorry you can't come," Suzanne said, and Ivy knew she was making progress. Still, it hurt her to see Gregory turn away.

She dawdled in the dressing room long enough for the others to go. When she came out, there were only two customers left, trying on hats and laughing.

Will was relaxing in a canvas chair with one leg propped up on a trunk, studying a photograph in his hands. He turned it facedown when he saw her. "Thanks for stopping by," he said.

"Will, you didn't give me a chance to tell you what I liked about your paintings. I couldn't find the right words at first—"

"I wasn't fishing for compliments, Ivy."

"I don't care whether you were or weren't," she said, and plopped down in the chair across from him. "I have something to say."

"All right." His mouth curved up slightly. "Shoot."

"It's about the one called *Too Soon.*"

127

Will took off his hat. She wished he had kept it on. Somehow—more and more, it seemed—looking into his eyes made it difficult for her to speak. She told herself they were just deep brown eyes, but whenever she looked into them she felt as if she were going into free fall.

The eyes are windows to the soul, she'd read once. And his were wide open.

She focused on her hands. "Sometimes, when something touches you, it's hard to find the words. You can say things like 'beautiful,' 'fabulous,' 'awesome,' but the words don't really describe how you feel, especially if you were feeling all that, but the picture made you—made you hurt some, too. And your picture did." She flexed her fingers. "That's all."

"Thanks," Will said.

She looked up at him then, which was a mistake.

"Ivy—"

She tried to look away, but couldn't.

"—how are you?"

"I'm fine. Really, I am." Why did she have to keep telling people that? And why, when she said it to Will, did it feel as if he could see straight through the lie?

"I have something to say, too," he told her. "Take care of yourself."

She could feel him looking at her cheek, the

one that had been bruised during the assault. There was still a pale wash of color there, though she had done her best to disguise it with makeup.

"Please take care of yourself."

"Why wouldn't I?" she snapped.

"Sometimes people don't."

Ivy wanted to say, You don't know what you're talking about, you've never lost anyone you loved. But then she remembered Gregory's words about Will having gone through a tough time. Maybe Will did understand.

"Who's the person in your painting?" Ivy asked. "Is it someone you knew?"

"My mother. My father still won't look at the picture." Then he waved that thought away and leaned forward. "Be careful, Ivy. Don't forget that there are other people who will feel that they have lost everything if they lose you."

Ivy looked away.

He reached for her face. She pulled back instinctively when he touched the bruised side. But he didn't hurt her, and he didn't let go. He cupped one hand around the back of her head. There was no escaping him.

Maybe she didn't want to escape him.

"Be careful, Ivy. Be careful!" His eyes shone with a strange intensity. "I'm telling you—*be careful!*"

Ivy blinked. Then she broke away from Will and ran.

9

Tristan lay back in the grass, exhausted. The park at the end of Main Street was filling up with people. Their picnic blankets looked like bright-colored rafts on a green sea. Kids rolled around and punched each other. Dogs pulled against their leashes and touched noses. Two teenagers kissed. An older couple flipped down their sunshades and watched, the woman smiling.

Lacey returned from her exploration of the park's stage, which was set up for the five o'clock performance. She dropped down next to Tristan. "It was a silly thing to do," she chided.

He had expected her to say something like that.

"Which part?" he asked. After all, the afternoon had been long and eventful.

"Trying to get inside Gregory's head." She

131

snorted. "It's a wonder he didn't knock you as far as Manhattan. Or L.A.!"

"I was desperate, Lacey! I've got to know what kind of game he's playing with Ivy and Suzanne."

"And you thought you needed a trip inside his head to find that out?" she asked incredulously. "You should have asked me. His game's no different than the kind I've seen a lot of guys play with girls. He's taking the easy one for a ride and chasing Miss Hard-to-Get." She moved her face close to Tristan's. "Am I right?"

Tristan didn't reply. It wasn't just a romantic game that was worrying him. Ever since he had made the connection between Caroline's death and Ivy's delivery to the house next door, he had wondered about the hidden purpose behind Gregory's new closeness to Ivy.

"Well, I hope you learned your lesson today," Lacey said.

"I have a pounding headache," he replied. "Are you satisfied?"

She laid her hand lightly on his forehead and said in a quieter voice, "If it makes you feel any better, Gregory probably has one, too."

Tristan squinted up at her, surprised by this small bit of gentleness.

She removed her hand and squinted back. "And why were you chasing Philip around, getting inside *his* mind?" she demanded. "Seems to me like another waste of energy. He already sees us glow—and gets in trouble every time he mentions it. That little conversation put Gregory in a *real* good mood this afternoon."

"I had to tell Philip who I was. Beth signed my name on the computer message. If Philip tells her he sees me, or my light, sooner or later she is going to have to believe."

Lacey shook her head doubtfully.

"And speaking of Philip," Tristan said, pulling himself up on one elbow, "I noticed how Gregory's mood got even better when Philip stopped talking about angels and pulled out an actual photograph of one. What mission were *you* working on today when you jumped into that picture?"

Lacey didn't answer him right away. She gazed up at three women in leotards who had just been introduced onstage. "What do you suppose they're going to do?"

"Dance or aerobics. Answer my question."

"If I were them, I'd wear veils."

"Try again," Tristan said.

"I was working on my semimaterializing process," she told him, "solidifying myself enough to show a general shape but not become an actual body. You never know—I might need to do something like that sometime in the future. To complete my mission, of course."

"Of course. And projecting your voice, so that everyone at Old West Photos could hear you—I guess you needed to practice that some more, too."

"Oh, well, that," she said with a flick of her hand. "I was working on *your* mission then."

"My mission?"

"In my own way," she replied. "You and I have very different styles."

"True. I'd never have thought of telling Will he has nice buns."

"Terrific buns," Lacey corrected him. "The best I've seen in a long time . . ." She looked at Tristan thoughtfully. "Roll over."

"No way."

She laughed, then said, "That chick of yours, she wears her skin like a suit of armor. I thought that if I got a little joke going, I could get her to loosen up some, to open up to Will. I thought I had a chance, since she couldn't see his eyes beneath his hat. I think it's his eyes that get to her, that make her shut down like that."

"She sees me in them," Tristan said.

"Some guys will do that to you," Lacey went on. "They've got eyes a girl can drown in."

"She doesn't know it, but she sees me in them."

When Lacey did not confirm this, he sat all

the way up. "Does Ivy see me looking out at her through Will's eyes?"

"No," Lacey said. "She sees another guy who's fallen in love with her, and it scares her to death."

"I don't believe it!" Tristan said. "You've got it wrong, Lacey."

"I've got it right."

"Will may have a crush, and she may find him sort of attractive, but—"

Lacey lay back in the grass. "Okay, okay. You're going to believe only what you want to believe, no matter what." She stuck one arm behind her head, propping it up a little. "Which isn't a whole lot different than the way Ivy believes—in spite of what's right in front of her nose."

"Ivy could never love anyone else," Tristan insisted. "I didn't know that before the accident, but I know it now. Ivy loves only me. I'm sure of that now."

Lacey tapped him on the arm with a long nail. "Excuse me for pointing out that you're dead now."

Tristan pulled his knees up and rested an arm on each one. He concentrated enough to materialize his fingertips, then dropped one of his hands and ripped up pieces of grass.

"You're getting good," Lacey observed. "That didn't take much effort."

He was too angry to acknowledge the compliment.

"Tristan, you're right. Ivy loves you, more than she loves anyone else. But the world goes on, and if you want her to stay alive, she can't stay in love with death. Life needs life. That's how the world goes."

Tristan didn't reply. He watched the three leotard ladies bounce around, then plod off the stage, shining with sweat. He listened to a little girl dressed like Annie half-sing, half-scream "Tomorrow, " over and over.

"It really doesn't matter who's right," he said at last. "I need Will. I can't help Ivy without him."

Lacey nodded. "He's just arrived. I guess he's taking a break from work—he's sitting by himself, not far from the park gate."

"The others are over there," Tristan said, pointing in the opposite direction.

Beth and Philip were lying on their stomachs on a big blanket, watching the performances and picking clover, weaving it into a long chain. Suzanne sat with Gregory on the same blanket, her arms wrapped around him from behind. She rested against his back, laying her chin on his shoulder. Eric had joined them, but was sitting on the grass just beyond the corner of the blanket, fidgeting with the end of it. He continually looked over the crowd, his body twitching at odd moments, his head turning to look quickly behind him.

136

They watched several more performances, then Ivy was introduced. Philip immediately stood up and clapped. Everyone started to laugh, including Ivy, who glanced over in his direction.

"That will help her," Lacey said. "It breaks the ice. I *like* that kid."

Ivy began to play, not the song she was scheduled to play, but "Moonlight Sonata," the music she had played for Tristan one night, a night that seemed as if it had been summers and summers ago.

This is for me, Tristan thought. This is what she played for me, he wanted to tell them all, the night she turned darkness into light, the night she danced with me. Ivy's playing for *me,* he wanted to tell Gregory and Will.

Gregory was sitting absolutely still, unaware of Suzanne's small movements, his eyes focused on Ivy as if he were spellbound.

Will also sat still in the grass, one knee up, his arm resting casually on it. But there was nothing casual about the way he listened and the way he watched her. He was drinking up every shimmering drop. Tristan rose to his feet and moved toward Will.

From Will's perspective Tristan watched Ivy, her strong hands, her tangle of gold hair in the late-afternoon sun, the expression on her face.

She was in a different world than he was, and he longed with his whole soul to be part of it. But she didn't know; he feared she would never know.

In the blink of an eye, Tristan matched thoughts with Will and slipped inside him. He heard Ivy's music through Will's ears now. When she had finished playing, he rose up with Will. He clapped and clapped, hands high above his head, high above Will's head. Ivy bowed and nodded, and glanced over at him.

Then she turned to the others. Suzanne, Beth, and Eric cheered. Philip jumped up and down, trying to see over the heads of the standing audience. Gregory stood still. Gregory and Ivy were the only two people in that noisy park standing motionless, silent, gazing at each other as if they had forgotten everyone else.

Will turned abruptly and walked back toward the street. Tristan slipped out of him and sank down on the grass. A few moments later he felt Lacey next to him. She didn't say anything, just sat with him, shoulder touching shoulder, like an old team member on the swim bench.

"I was wrong, Lacey," Tristan said. "And so were you. Ivy doesn't see me. Ivy doesn't see Will, either."

"She sees Gregory," Lacey said.

"Gregory," he repeated bitterly. "I don't know how I can save her now!"

In a way, dealing with Suzanne after the performance had been easier than Ivy expected. As planned earlier, Ivy met Philip and her friends by the park gate. Before she got a chance to greet them, Suzanne turned away.

Ivy reached out and touched her friend on the arm. "How did you like Will's paintings?" she asked.

Suzanne acted as if she hadn't heard.

"Suzanne, Ivy was wondering what you thought of Will's paintings," Beth said softly.

The response came slowly. "I'm sorry, Beth, what did you just say?"

Beth glanced uneasily from Suzanne to Ivy. Eric laughed, enjoying the strain between the girls. Gregory seemed preoccupied and distant from both Suzanne and Ivy.

"We were talking about Will's paintings," Beth prompted.

"They're great," Suzanne said. She had her shoulder and head turned at an angle that cut Ivy out of her view.

Ivy waited for some kids with balloons to pass, then shifted her position and made another attempt to talk to Suzanne. This time she got Suzanne's back in her face. Beth stood between the two girls and began to chatter, as if words could fill up the silence and distance between them.

As soon as Beth paused for breath, Ivy said she had to go, so that she could get Philip to his friend's house on time. Perhaps Philip saw and understood more than Ivy had realized. He waited until they were a block away from the others before he said, "Sammy just got back from camp and said not to come till after seven o'clock."

Ivy laid her hand on his shoulder. "I know. Thanks for not mentioning it."

On their way to the car, Ivy stopped at a small stand and purchased two bouquets of poppies. Philip didn't ask her why she bought them or where they were going. Maybe he had figured that out, too.

As Ivy drove away from the festival she felt surprisingly lighter. She had tried hard to reassure Suzanne, to please her friend by keeping her distance from Gregory. She had reached out to Suzanne several times, but each time her hand had been slapped back. There was no reason to keep trying now, to keep tiptoeing around Suzanne and Gregory. Her anger turned to relief; she felt suddenly free of a burden she hadn't wanted to carry.

"Why do we have two bouquets?" Philip asked as Ivy drove along, humming. "Is one of them going to be from me?"

He had guessed.

"Actually, they're both from us. I thought it would be nice to leave some flowers on Caroline's grave."

"Why?"

Ivy shrugged. "Because she was Gregory's mother, and Gregory has been good to both of us."

"But she was a nasty lady."

Ivy glanced over at him. *Nasty* wasn't one of the words in Philip's vocabulary. "What?"

"Sammy's mother said she was nasty."

"Well, Sammy's mother doesn't know everything," Ivy replied, driving through the large iron gates.

"She knew Caroline," Philip said stubbornly.

Ivy was aware that a lot of people hadn't liked Caroline. Gregory himself had never spoken well of his mother.

"All right, here's what we'll do," she said as she parked the car. "We'll make one bouquet, the orange one, from me to Caroline, and the other, the purple one, from me and you to Tristan."

They walked silently to the wealthy area of Riverstone Rise.

When Ivy went to lay the flowers on Caroline's grave, she noticed that Philip hung back.

"Is it cold?" he called to her.

"Cold?"

"Sammy's sister says that mean people have cold graves."

141

"It's very warm. And look, someone has left Caroline a long-stemmed red rose, someone who must have loved her very much."

Philip wasn't convinced and looked anxious to get away. Ivy wondered if he was going to act funny around Tristan's grave, too. But as they walked toward it he started hopping over the stones and turned back into his old cheerful, chatterbox self.

"Remember how Tristan put the salad in his hair at Mom's wedding," Philip asked, "and it was all runny? And remember the celery he stuck in his ears?"

"And the shrimp tails in his nose," Ivy said.

"And those black things on his teeth."

"Olives. I remember."

It was the first time since the funeral that Philip had spoken to her about Tristan, the Tristan he had once played with. She wondered why her brother was suddenly able to do so.

"And remember how I beat him at checkers?"

"Two out of three games," she said.

"Yeah." Philip grinned to himself, then took off.

He ran up to the last mausoleum in a row of the elegant burial houses and knocked on the door. "Open up in there!" he shouted, then flapped his arms and flew ahead of Ivy, waiting for her at the next turn.

"Tristan was good at Sega Genesis," Philip said.

"He taught you some cool tricks, didn't he?"

"Yep. I miss him."

"Me, too," Ivy said, biting her lip. She was glad that Philip had rushed ahead again. She didn't want to ruin his happy memories with tears.

At Tristan's grave Ivy knelt down and ran her fingers over the letters on the stone—Tristan's name and dates. She could not say the small prayer that had been carved on the stone, a prayer that put him in the hands of the angels, so her fingers read it silently. Philip also touched the stone, then he arranged the flowers. He wanted to shape them into a *T.*

He's healing, Ivy thought as she watched him. If he can, maybe I can, too.

"Tristan will like these when he comes back," Philip said, standing up to admire his own work.

Ivy thought she had misunderstood her brother.

"I hope he gets back before the flowers die," he continued.

"What?"

"Maybe he'll come back when it's dark."

Ivy put her hand over her mouth. She didn't want to deal with this, but somebody had to, and she knew that she couldn't count on her mother.

"Where do you think Tristan is now?" Ivy asked cautiously.

"I know where he is. At the festival."

"And how do you know that?"

"He told me. He's my angel, Ivy. I know you said never to say *angel* again"—Philip was talking very fast, as if he could avoid her anger by saying the word quickly—"but that's what he is. I didn't know it was him till he told me today."

Ivy rubbed her hands over her bare arms.

"He must still be there with that other one," Philip said.

"That other one?" she repeated.

"The other angel," he said softly. Then he reached in his pocket and pulled out a creased photograph. It was a picture of them that had been taken at Old West Photos, but not the same one she had been given. Something had gone wrong with the developer, or perhaps the film itself. There was a cloudiness behind him.

Philip pointed to it. "That's her. The other angel."

Its shape vaguely resembled a girl, so Ivy could see why he might say that.

"Where did you get this?"

"Will gave it to me. I asked him for it because she didn't get into the picture he gave you. I think she's a friend of Tristan's."

Ivy could only imagine what Philip's active

mind would create next—an entire community of angel friends and relatives. "Tristan is dead," she said. "Dead. Do you understand?"

"Yes." His face was somber and knowing as an adult's, but his skin looked baby smooth and golden in the evening sun. At that moment he reminded Ivy of a painting of an angel.

"I miss Tristan the way he used to be," Philip told her. "I wish he could still play with me. Sometimes I still feel like crying. But I'm glad he's my angel now, Ivy. He'll help you too."

She didn't argue. She couldn't reason with a kid who believed as strongly as Philip did.

"We need to go," she said at last.

He nodded, then threw his head back and shouted, "I hope you like it, Tristan."

Ivy hurried ahead of him. She was glad she was dropping him off at Sammy's for a sleepover. With Sammy back, maybe Philip would spend more time in the real world.

When Ivy arrived home she found a note from her mother reminding her that she and Andrew had gone to the dinner gala that was part of the arts festival.

"Good," Ivy said aloud. She'd had enough strained conversations for one day. An evening with just Ella and a good book was exactly what she needed. She ran upstairs, kicked off her shoes, and changed into her favorite T-shirt, which was full of holes and so big she could wear it like a short dress.

"It's just you and me, cat," Ivy said to Ella, who had chased her up the steps and down again to the kitchen. "Is mademoiselle ready to dine?" Ivy set two cans out on the counter. "For you, seafood nuggets. For me, tuna. I hope I don't get them mixed up."

Ella rubbed back and forth against Ivy's legs as Ivy prepared the food. Then the cat mewed softly.

"Why the fancy dishes, you ask?" Ivy got down a matched set of cut-glass plates, along with a crystal drinking glass and a crystal bowl. "We're celebrating. I played the piece, Ella, I played the movement all the way through!"

Ella mewed again.

"No, not the one I've been practicing—and not the one you've been practicing, either. The 'Moonlight.' That's right." Ivy sighed. "I guess I had to play it for him one last time before I could play for myself again. I think I could play anything now! Come on, cat."

Ella followed her into the family room and watched curiously as Ivy lit a candle and put it on the floor between them. "Is this classy, or what?"

The cat let out another soft meow.

Ivy opened the large French doors that led out to the patio at the back of the house, then put on a CD of some soft jazz.

"Some cats don't have Saturday nights like this, you know."

Ella purred through dinner. Ivy felt just as content as she watched Ella clean herself, then settle down by the tall screen doors, her nose and ears positioned to catch all the smells and tiny sounds of twilight.

After a few minutes of keeping vigil with Ella, Ivy dug a book out from underneath the chair cushion, a collection of stories Gregory had been reading. Moving the candle out of the draft, she rolled over on her stomach next to it and began to read.

It wasn't till then that she realized how tired she was. The words kept blurring before her eyes, and the candle cast a hypnotic flicker across the page. The story was some kind of mystery, and she tried to concentrate, not wanting to miss any of the clues. But before the killer struck a second time, her eyes closed.

Ivy didn't know how long she had been sleeping. It had been a dreamless sleep. Her mind had jerked awake suddenly, alerted by some sound.

Before she opened her eyes, she knew that it was late. The CD had ended and she could hear the crickets outside, a full choir of them. From the dining room came the soft bonging of the mantel clock. She lost count of the hours—eleven? twelve?

Without lifting her head, she opened her eyes in the dark room and saw that the candle, though still burning, was a stub. Ella had left, and one screen door gaped open, silvery in the moonlight.

A cool breeze blew in. The fine hairs along Ivy's arms stirred, and her skin felt suddenly chill. It was Ella who had slipped through the door, she told herself. Probably the screen had been unlatched, and Ella pushed it open to let herself out. But the draft was strong, drawn across the room to the door behind Ivy. That door, which led to the gallery, had been closed when Ivy fell asleep.

It was open now—without turning around, she knew it. And she knew that someone was there watching her. A board creaked in the doorway, then another, much closer to her. She could feel his dark presence hovering above her.

Ivy quietly sucked in her breath, then opened her mouth and screamed.

10

Ivy screamed and fought him, kicking behind her with all her strength. He held her down on the floor, his hand pressed over her nose and mouth. She screamed into his hand, then she tried to bite it, but he was too quick for her. She started rolling her body back and forth. She'd roll him into the candle flame if she had to.

"Ivy! Ivy! It's me! Be quiet, Ivy! You'll scare Philip. It's just me."

She went limp beneath him. "Gregory."

He slowly lifted himself off her. They stared at each other, sweating and out of breath.

"I thought you were asleep," he said. "I was trying to see if you were all right without waking you."

"I—I just—I didn't know who you were. Philip is out. He's staying over at Sammy's tonight, and Mom and Andrew are at the gala."

"Everybody's out?" Gregory asked sharply.

"Yes, and I thought—"

Gregory rammed his fist into his palm several times, then stopped when he saw the way she was looking at him.

"What's wrong with you?" he demanded. "What's wrong with you, Ivy?" He held her by both arms. "How can you be so stupid?"

"What do you mean?" she asked.

He stared deep into her eyes. "Why have you been avoiding me?"

Ivy looked away.

"Look at me! Answer me!"

She swung her head back. "Ask Suzanne, if you want to know why."

She saw the flicker in his eyes then, as if he suddenly understood. It was hard to believe that he hadn't guessed what was going on. Why else would she avoid him?

He loosened his grip. "Ivy." His voice was softer now, wavering. "You're home alone, late at night, in a house where you were attacked last week, with the door wide open. You left the door wide open! Why would you do something so dumb?"

Ivy swallowed hard. "I thought the screen was latched. But it wasn't, I guess, and Ella must have pushed it open."

Gregory leaned back against the sofa, rubbing his head.

"I'm sorry. I'm sorry I upset you," she said.

He took a deep breath and laid one hand over hers. He was much calmer now. "No, I scared you. I should be the one apologizing."

Even in the flickering candlelight, Ivy could see the weariness around his eyes. She reached up and touched the temple he had been rubbing. "Headache?"

"It's not as bad as it was earlier today."

"But it still hurts. Lie down," she said. She set a pillow on the floor for his head. "I'll get you some tea and aspirin."

"I can get it myself."

"Let me." She put her hand lightly on his shoulder. "You've done so much for me, Gregory. Please let me do this for you."

"I haven't done anything I didn't want to."

"Please."

He lay back.

Ivy got up and put on a disk with sax and piano music. "Too loud? Too soft?"

"Perfect," he said, closing his eyes.

She made a pot of tea, put some cookies on the tray along with aspirin, and brought it back to the candlelit room.

They sipped awhile in silence and munched

cookies. Then Gregory playfully clinked his cup against hers in a silent toast.

"What is this stuff? I feel like I'm drinking a garden."

She laughed. "You are—and it's good for you."

He took another sip and looked at her through the wispy steam. "You're good for me," he said.

"Do you like to have your back scratched?" Ivy asked. "Philip loves to."

"Have it scratched?"

"Rubbed. When you were a little boy, didn't your mother ever rub your back trying to get you to sleep?"

"*My* mother?"

"Turn over."

He looked at her, somewhat amused, then set down his tea and rolled over on his stomach.

Ivy began to rub his back, running her hand over it in small and big circles, the way she did with Philip. She could feel the tension in him; every muscle was tight. What Gregory really needed was a massage, and it would feel better if he removed his shirt, but she was afraid to suggest this.

Why? He's just my stepbrother, Ivy reminded herself. He's not a date. He's a good friend and kind of a brother—

"Ivy?"

"Yes?"

"Would it be all right with you if I took off my shirt?"

"It would be better," she said.

He removed it and lay down again. His back was long and tan and strong from playing tennis. She began to work again, pushing hard this time, moving her hands up his spine and across his muscular shoulders. Ivy kneaded the back of his neck, her fingers working up into his dark hair, then she ran her hands down to his lower spine. Slowly but surely she felt him relax beneath her fingers.

Without warning he rolled over and looked up at her.

In the candlelight, his features cast rugged shadows. Golden light filled a little hollow in his neck. She was tempted to touch that hollow, to lay her hand on his neck and feel where his pulse jumped.

"You know," Gregory said, "last winter, when my father told me he was marrying Maggie, the last thing I wanted was you in my house."

"I know," Ivy replied, smiling down at him.

He reached up and touched her on the cheek.

"Now . . ." he said, spreading his fingers, letting them get tangled in her hair. "Now . . ." He pulled her head down closer to his.

If we kiss, thought Ivy, if we kiss and Suzanne—

"Now?" he whispered.

She couldn't fight it anymore. She closed her eyes.

With both hands, he pulled her face swiftly down to his. Then his rough hands relaxed, and the kiss was long and light and delicious. He lifted her face and kissed her softly on the throat.

Ivy moved her mouth down and they started kissing again. Then they both froze, startled by the sound of a motor and the sweep of headlights on the driveway outside. Andrew's car.

Gregory rolled his head back and laughed a little. "Unbelievable." He sighed. "Our chaperons have arrived."

Ivy felt how slowly and reluctantly his fingers let her go. Then she blew out the candle, turned on the light, and tried not to think about Suzanne.

Tristan wished he knew some way to soothe Ivy. Her sheets were twisted and her hair a tangle of gold that had been tossed back and forth. Had she been dreaming again? Had something happened since he left her at the festival?

After the performance, Tristan knew he had to find out who wanted to hurt Ivy. He also knew he was running out of time. If Ivy fell for Gregory, then Tristan would lose Will as a way of reaching her and warning her.

Ivy stirred. "Who's there? Who's there?" she murmured.

Tristan recognized the beginning of the dream. A sense of dread washed over him, as if he himself were being drawn into the nightmare. He couldn't stand to see her that frightened again. If only he could hold her, if only he could take her in his arms—

Ella, where was Ella?

The cat sat purring in the window. Tristan quickly moved toward her, materializing his fingers. He marveled at his growing strength, how he could pick up the cat by the scruff of her neck for a few seconds and carry her to the bed. He put her down and, just before the strength went out of him, used his fingertips to nudge Ivy awake.

"Ella," she said softly. "Oh, Ella." Her arms wrapped around the cat.

Tristan stepped back from the bed. This was how he had to love her now, one step removed from her, helping others to comfort and care for her in his place.

With Ella snuggled next to her, Ivy settled into a more peaceful sleep. The dream was gone, pushed deeper into the recesses of her mind, deep enough not to trouble her for a while. If only he could get to that dream. Tristan was sure that Ivy had seen something she shouldn't have the night Caroline died—or that someone thought she had seen something. If he knew what it was, he'd know who was after her. But he couldn't get inside her any more than he could get inside Gregory.

He left her sleeping there. He had already decided what to do, and planned to do it in spite of all of Lacey's warnings: time-travel back in Eric's mind. He had to find out if Eric was the one riding his motorcycle through Ivy's dream, and if he had been to Caroline's the evening she died.

As Tristan moved toward Eric's house he tried to recall all the details he had seen earlier that night. After the festival, Lacey had accompanied him to Caroline's house. While she had opened closets, looked behind pictures, and poked through things that were in the process of being boxed up, he'd studied the details of the house, outside and in. These would be the keys, the objects he could meditate on once inside someone's head, giving him his chance to trigger the right string of memories.

"If you're going to go through with this stupid plan of yours," Lacey had said while digging between the sofa cushions, "go prepared. And get some rest first."

"I'm ready now," he had argued, his glance sweeping the living room where Caroline had died.

"Listen, jock angel," Lacey replied, "you're starting to feel your strength now. That's good, but don't let yourself get carried away. You're not ready for the heavenly Olympics, not yet. If you insist on trying to slip inside Eric, then get some hours of darkness tonight. You'll need it."

Tristan hadn't answered her right away. Standing by the picture window, he had noticed that there was a clear view of the street and anyone coming up the walk. "Maybe you're right," he'd said at last.

"No maybe about it. Besides, Eric will be most vulnerable to you at dawn or just after, when he's sleeping lightly," she had told him. "Try to get him just conscious enough to follow your suggestion, but not so awake that he realizes what he's doing."

It had sounded like good advice. Now, with the sky starting to glow in the east, Tristan found Eric asleep on the floor of his bedroom. The bed was still made, and Eric was still dressed in his clothes from the day before, lying on his side, curled in a corner next to his stereo. Magazines were scattered nearby. Tristan knelt down next to him. Materializing his fingers, he paged through a motorcycle magazine till he found a picture of a machine similar to Eric's. He focused on it and nudged Eric awake.

Tristan was admiring the cycle's clean, curved

lines, imagining its power, and suddenly he knew he was seeing it through Eric's eyes. It had been as easy as slipping inside Will. Maybe Lacey was wrong, he thought. Maybe she didn't realize just how well he had developed his powers. Then the picture softened at the edges.

Eric's eyes shut. For a moment there was nothing but dark around Tristan. Now was the time for him to think about Caroline's street, to take Eric on a slow ride up to her house, to get him started on a memory.

But suddenly the blackness opened out, as if a dark wall had been unzipped, and Tristan went hurtling forward. Road came at him out of nowhere and kept coming like the road in a video racing game. He was moving too quickly to respond, too quickly to guess where he was going.

He was on a motorcycle, racing over a road through brilliant flashes of light and dark. He lifted his eyes from the road and saw trees and stone walls and houses. The trees were so intensely green they burned against Tristan's eyes. The blue sky was neon. Red felt like heat.

They were racing up a road, climbing higher and higher. Tristan tried to slow them down, to steer one way, then another, to exert some control, but he was powerless.

Suddenly they screeched to a halt. Tristan looked up and saw the Baines house.

Gregory's home—it was and it wasn't. He stared at the house as they walked toward it. It was like looking at a room reflected in a Christmas ornament; he saw objects he knew well stretched by a strange perspective, at once familiar and weird.

Was he in a dream, or was this a memory whose edges had been burned and curled by drugs?

They knocked, then walked through the front door. There was no ceiling, no roof. In fact, there wasn't a furnished room, but a huge playground, whose fence was the shell of the house. Gregory was there, looking down at them from the top of a very tall sliding board, a silver chute that did not stop at ground level but tunneled into it.

There was a woman also. Caroline, Tristan realized suddenly.

When she saw them she waved and smiled in a warm and friendly way. Gregory stayed on top of his sliding board, looking down at them coldly, but Caroline beckoned them over to a merry-go-round, and they could not resist.

She was on one side, they were on the other. They ran and pushed, ran and pushed, then hopped on. They whirled around and around, but instead of slowing down, as Tristan expected, they went faster and faster. And faster and faster still—they hung by their fingertips as they spun. Tristan thought his head would fly off. Then their fingers slipped and they went hurtling into space.

When Tristan looked up, the world still spun for a moment, then stopped. The playground had disappeared, but the shell of the house remained, enclosing a cemetery.

He saw his own grave. He saw Caroline's. Then he saw a third grave, gaping open, a pile of freshly dug earth next to it.

Was it Eric who started shaking then, or was it himself? Tristan didn't know, and he couldn't stop it—he shook violently and fell to the ground. The ground rumbled and tilted. Gravestones rolled around him, rolled like teeth shaken out of a skull. He was on his side, shaking, curled in a ball, waiting for the earth to crack, to split like a mouth and swallow him.

Then it stopped. Everything was still. He saw in front of him a glossy picture of a motorcycle. Eric had awakened.

It was a dream, thought Tristan. He was still inside, but Eric didn't seem to notice. Maybe he was too exhausted, or maybe his fried brain was too used to strange feelings and thoughts to respond to Tristan.

Did the bizarre events of the dream mean anything? Was there some truth hidden in them, or were they the wanderings of a druggie's mind?

Caroline was a mysterious figure. He remembered how they had no will to resist her invitation to a ride on the merry-go-round. Her face was so welcoming.

He saw it again, the welcoming face. It was older now. He imagined her standing at the door of her own house. Then he walked through that door with her. This time he was in Eric's memory!

Caroline looked around the room, and they did, too. The blinds were opened in the big picture window; he could see dark clouds gathering in the western sky. In a vase was a long-stemmed rose, still tightly curled in a bud. Caroline was sitting across from him, smiling at him. Now she was frowning.

The memory jumped, like a badly spliced movie, frames dropping out of it. Smiling, frowning, smiling again. Tristan could barely hear the words being spoken; they were drowned out by waves of emotion.

Caroline threw back her head and laughed. She laughed almost hysterically, and Tristan felt an overwhelming sense of fear and frustration. She laughed and laughed, and Tristan thought he'd explode with the force of Eric's frustration.

He grabbed Caroline's arms and shook her, shook her so hard her head rolled backward and forward like a rag doll's. Suddenly he heard the words being screamed out at her:

"Listen to me. I mean it! It's not a joke. Nobody's laughing but you. It's not a joke!"

Then Tristan felt a pressure squeezing his head, compressing his mind so intensely he thought he would dissolve. Caroline and the room dissolved, like a scene from a movie disintegrating in front of his eyes; the screen went black. Eric had pressed down on the memory. His own bedroom suddenly came back into focus.

Tristan got up and moved with Eric across the room. He watched his fingers open a knapsack and pull out an envelope. Eric shook brightly colored pills into his quivering hand, lifted them to his mouth, and swallowed.

Now, Tristan thought, was the time to take seriously Lacey's warnings about a drug-poisoned mind. He cut out of there fast.

11

"Capes and teeth are selling big," Betty said, glancing through the sales receipts for 'Tis the Season. "Is there a convention for vampires at the Hilton this week?"

"Don't know," Ivy murmured, counting out a customer's change for the third time.

"I think you need a break, dear," Lillian observed.

Ivy glanced at the clock. "I just had dinner an hour ago."

"I know," said Lillian, "but since you'll be closing up for Bet and me, and since you just sold that sweet young man who bought the Dracula cape a pair of wax lips . . ."

"Wax lips? Are you sure?"

"The Ruby Reds," Lillian said. "Don't worry, I caught him at the door and got him to trade them for a nice set of fangs. But I do think you should take a little break."

Ivy stared down at the cash register, embarrassed. She had been making mistakes for three days now, though the sisters had graciously pretended not to notice. She wondered if the cash box had come out right Sunday and Monday. She was amazed that they would trust her to close up that night.

"The last time I saw you like this," Betty said, "you were falling in love."

Lillian shot her sister a look.

"I'm not this time," Ivy said firmly. "But maybe I could use a break."

"Off you go," Lillian said. "Take as long as you need."

She gave Ivy a gentle push.

Ivy walked the top floor of the mall from one end to the other, trying once more to sort things out. Since Saturday she and Gregory had been doing a sort of shy dance around each other: hands brushing, eyes meeting, greeting each other softly, then backing away. Sunday night her mother had set the table for a family dinner and lit two candles. Gregory looked at Ivy from across the table as he'd often done before, but this time Ivy saw the flame dancing in his eyes. Monday Gregory had slipped away without speaking to anyone. Ivy didn't know where he had gone and didn't dare ask. Maybe to Suzanne's. Maybe Saturday night had been just a moment of closeness—a single moment, a single kiss, after all the hard times they had shared.

Ivy felt guilty.

But was it so wrong, caring for someone who cared for her? Was it wrong, wanting to touch someone who touched her gently? Was it wrong, changing her mind about Gregory?

Ivy had never felt so mixed up. Only one thing was clear: she was going to have to get her act together and concentrate on what she doing, she told herself—just as she ran into a baby stroller.

"Oops. Sorry."

The woman pushing the stroller smiled, and Ivy returned the smile, then backed into a cart selling earrings and chains. Everything jingled.

"Sorry. Sorry."

She narrowly avoided a trash can, then headed straight for the Coffee Mill.

Ivy took her cup of cappuccino to the far end of the mall. The two big stores that had been there were closed, and several lights had burned out. She sat on an empty bench in the artificial twilight, sipping her drink. Voices from shoppers at the other end of the mall lapped toward her in soft waves that never quite reached her.

Ivy closed her eyes for a moment, enjoying the solitude. Then she opened them, turning her head quickly, surprised by three distinct voices to the right of her. One of them was very familiar.

"It's all there," he said.

"I'm going to count it."

"Don't you trust me?"

"I said I'm going to count it. You figure out whether I trust you."

In a dimly lit tunnel that led to the parking garage, Gregory, Eric, and a third person were talking, unaware that anyone was watching. When the third person turned his head into the light, Ivy could hardly believe her eyes. She had seen him outside the school and knew he was a drug dealer. But when she saw Gregory hand the dealer a bag, what she really couldn't believe was how she had forgotten about the other side of Gregory.

How had she gotten so close to a guy whose friends were rich and fast? How had she come to rely on someone who, bored with what he had, took stupid risks? Why did she trust a person who played dangerous games with his friends, no matter who it hurt?

Tristan had warned her once, before that night at the train bridges, before the night that Will was almost killed. But Ivy thought that Gregory had changed since then. In the last four weeks he'd— Well, obviously, she was wrong.

She got up abruptly from the bench, spilling cappuccino down the front of her.

Tristan! she cried out silently. Help me, Tristan! Help me get my head straight!

She ran down the hall to the brighter area of the mall. She was hurrying for the escalator when she slammed into Will.

The girl with him, an auburn-haired girl whom Ivy recognized from Eric's party, swore softly.

Will stared at Ivy, and she stared back. She could hardly stand it, the way he looked at her, the way he could hold her captive with his eyes.

"What are you doing here?" Ivy demanded.

"What's it to you?" the girl snapped.

Ivy ignored her. "Don't tell me," she said to Will, "you just had the feeling, you just thought—somehow you just knew—"

She saw a flicker of light in his eyes, and she glanced away quickly.

The girl with him was squinching up her face, looking at Ivy as if she were crazy; Ivy *felt* a little crazy. "I—I have to get to work," she said, but he held her still with his eyes.

"If you need me," Will told her, "call me." Then he turned his head slightly, as if someone had spoken over his shoulder.

Ivy brushed past him and hurried up the escalator, climbing faster than the steps moved, and rushed to the shop.

"Oh, dear," Lillian said when Ivy burst through the door.

"Oh, my!" said Betty.

Ivy was panting, from anger as much as running. Now she stopped to look down the front of her pale green dress. It was mud-colored.

"We should soak that right away."

"No, it's okay," she said, trying to catch her breath, breathing slowly and deeply to calm herself down. "I'll just sponge it off." She moved toward the rest room in the back, but Betty was already going through one rack of costumes, and Lillian was gazing thoughtfully at another.

"I'll just sponge it off," Ivy repeated. "I'll be out in a minute."

Lillian and Betty hummed to themselves.

"It's an old dress anyway," Ivy added.

Sometimes the old ladies played deaf.

"Something simple," she finally begged. Last time she had ended up as an alien—enhanced with batteries that made her blink and beep.

The sisters did keep it simple, giving her a soft white blouse, gathered and worn off the shoulders, and a colorful skirt.

"Oh, what a lovely gypsy she makes," Lillian said to Betty.

"We should dress her up every day," Betty agreed.

They smiled at her like two doting great-aunts.

"Don't forget to turn out the light in the back,

love," Betty said, then the sisters went home to their seven cats.

Ivy breathed a sigh of relief. She was glad to be running the shop alone for the next two hours. It kept her busy enough to keep her mind off what she had just seen.

She was angry—but at herself more than at Gregory. He was who he was. He hadn't changed his ways. It was she who had made him into the perfect guy.

At 9:25, Ivy was finished with her last customer. The mall had become virtually empty. Five minutes later she dimmed the lights in the shop, locked the door from the inside, and started counting the money and adding up receipts.

She was startled by someone knocking on the glass. "Gypsy girl," he called.

"Gregory."

For a moment she considered leaving him out there, putting back the glass wall that he had erected between them last January. She walked toward him slowly, unlatched the store door, and cracked it open three inches.

"Am I disturbing you?" he asked.

"I have to total the register and close up."

"I'll keep quiet," he promised.

Ivy opened the door a few inches more and he entered.

She started toward the cash register, then

turned back quickly. "I may as well get this out of the way now," she said.

Gregory waited; he looked as if he knew something big was coming.

"I saw you and Eric and the other guy—that dealer—making an exchange."

"Oh, that," he said, as if it were nothing.

"Oh, that?" she repeated.

"I thought you were going to tell me something like, from now on, we were never to see each other alone."

Ivy looked down, pulling and twisting a tassel on her skirt. It would probably be better if they didn't.

"Oh," he said, "I see. You were going to say that, too."

Ivy didn't answer him. She didn't honestly know.

Gregory walked over to her and laid his hand on top of hers, keeping her from yanking off the tassel.

"Eric does drugs," he said, "you know that. And he's gotten himself in deep, real deep, with our friendly neighborhood dealer. I bailed him out."

Ivy looked up into Gregory's eyes. Against his tan, they looked lighter, like a silver sea on a misty day.

"I don't blame you, Ivy, for thinking I'm

doing the wrong thing. If I thought Eric would stop when he ran out of money, I wouldn't pay up for him. But he won't stop, and they'll go after him."

He let go of her hand. "Eric's my friend. He's been my friend since grade school. I don't know what else to do."

Ivy turned away, thinking about how loyal Gregory was to Eric and how disloyal she had been to Suzanne.

"Go ahead. Say it," Gregory challenged her. "You don't like what I'm doing. You think I should find myself better friends."

She shook her head. "I don't blame you for what you're doing," she said. "Eric's lucky to have you for a friend, as lucky as I am. As lucky as Suzanne is."

He turned her face toward him with just one finger. "Finish up your work," he said, "and we can talk some more. We'll go out somewhere, not home, okay?"

"Okay."

"Are you going to wear that?" he asked, smiling.

"Oh! I forgot. I spilled cappuccino on my dress. It's soaking in the basin."

He laughed. "I don't mind. You look . . . uh, exotic," he said, his eyes dropping down to her bare shoulders.

She tingled a little.

"I guess I'll have to find a costume for me."

He started looking over the wall of hats and wigs. A few minutes later he called out to her, "How's this?"

Ivy looked up from behind the register and laughed out loud.

He was wearing a frizzy red wig, a top hat, and a polka-dotted bow tie.

"Dashing," she said.

Gregory tried on one costume after another— a Klingon mask, King Kong's head and chest, a huge flowered hat and boa.

"Clown!" said Ivy.

He grinned at her and waved his feathery stole.

"If you want to try on a whole outfit, there are fitting rooms in the back. The one on the left is large, with mirrors everywhere. You get all angles," she told him. "I'm really sorry Philip isn't here to play with you."

"When you're done, you can play with me," Gregory replied.

Ivy worked a little longer. When she finally closed the books, she saw that he had disappeared into the back.

"Gregory?" she called.

"Yes, my sveet," he answered with an accent.

"What are you doing?"

172

"Come here, my sveet," he replied. "I've been vaiting for you."

She smiled to herself. "What are you up to?"

Ivy tiptoed to the dressing room and slowly pushed open the swinging door. Gregory had flattened himself against the wall. Now he turned quickly, jumping in front of her.

"Oh!" she gasped. She wasn't acting; Gregory made a startlingly handsome vampire in a white shirt with a deep V-neck and a high-collared black cape. His dark hair was slicked back, and his eyes danced with mischief.

"Hello, my sveet."

"Tell me," she said, recovering from the surprise, "if you put in your fangs, will you be able to pronounce *w*'s?"

"No vay. Thees is how I speak." He pulled her into the room. "And may I say, my sveet, vat a lovely neck you have!"

Ivy laughed. He put in his long teeth and began to nuzzle her neck, tickling her.

"Where do I thrust in the wooden stake?" she asked, pushing him back a little. "Right there?" She poked him lightly where his shirt gaped.

Gregory caught her hand and held it for a long moment. Then he took out his teeth and lifted her hand to his mouth, kissing it softly. He pulled her closer to him. "I think you've already done it, thrust it straight through my heart," he told her.

Ivy looked up at him, barely breathing. His eyes burned like gray coals beneath his lowered lashes.

"What a lovely neck," he said, bending his head, his dark hair falling forward. He kissed her softly on the throat. He kissed her again and again, slowly moving his mouth up to hers.

His kisses became more insistent. Ivy answered with gentler kisses. He pressed her to him, held her tightly, then suddenly released her, dropping down before her. He knelt in front of her, reaching up to her, his strong, caressing hands moving slowly over her body, pulling her down to him. "It's okay," he said softly. "It's okay."

They clung to each other and swayed. Then Ivy opened her eyes. To the left, to the right, reflected in front of her, reflected from behind her—from every angle in the mirrored dressing room—she could see herself and Gregory wrapped around each other.

She pulled herself free of him. "No!" Her hands went up to her face, covering her eyes.

Gregory tried to pull her hands away from her face. She turned to the wall, cowering in the corner, but she couldn't get away from the reflection of the girl who had been kissing Gregory.

"This isn't right," she said.

"Isn't *right?*"

"It isn't a good thing. For you, or me, or Suzanne."

"Forget Suzanne! What matters is you and me."

"Don't forget Suzanne," Ivy pleaded softly. "She's wanted you for a long time. And I, I want to be near you, I want to talk to you, I want to touch you. And kiss you. How could I help it, when you've been so wonderful to me? But, Gregory, I know—" She took a deep breath. "I know I'm still in love with Tristan."

"And you think I *don't* know that?" He laughed. "You've made it kind of obvious, Ivy."

He took a step closer to her and reached out for her hand. "I know you're still in love with him and still hurting for him. Let me help ease the pain."

He held her hand softly in both of his.

"Think about it, Ivy. Just think about it," he said.

She nodded silently, her free hand toying with the tassel on her skirt.

"I'll change my clothes now," he told her, "and we'll go home in our own cars. I'll take a long route so we don't arrive at the same time. We won't even see each other going up to our rooms. So—" He lifted her hand to his mouth. "This is my good-night kiss," he said, gently touching his lips to her fingertips.

When Tristan awoke, only his soft glow lit the dressing room, shining back at him from each of the mirrors. But the darkness that he felt surrounding him in the empty room was more than the absence of light. The darkness felt like something real in itself, a soft and ominous shape, a presence that angered and frightened Tristan.

"Gregory," he said aloud, and the scenes he had witnessed hours earlier flashed through his mind. For a moment he thought the room was lit. Had Gregory really fallen in love with Ivy? Tristan wondered. And was he telling the truth about Eric and the dealer? Tristan had to know, had to get inside his head. "You're next, Gregory," he said. "You're next."

"Would you stop talking to yourself? How's a girl supposed to get her beauty sleep?"

Tristan pushed through the dressing room door into the shop, which was lit by two dim night-lights and an exit sign. Lacey was stretched out at the feet of King Kong.

"I waited for you at your Riverstone Rise condo," she said, then held up a dead flower. "Brought you this. There were others, just as dead, forming a *T* on your grave. Figured you hadn't been there for a while."

"I haven't."

"I checked out Eric," she continued, "just in case you'd gotten lost in that fun house otherwise known as his mind. Then I checked out Ivy, who's not having a good night—so what else is new?"

"Is she okay?" Tristan asked. He had wanted to follow her home and get the rest he needed there. Then he could have made sure that Ella was close by; he could have summoned Philip if she needed him. But he knew if he had gone with her, he'd have stayed up all night watching. "Is she okay?"

"She's Ivy," Lacey replied, fluffing up her hair. "So tell me, what did I miss in this soap opera? Gregory's just as restless as she is. What's eating him?"

Tristan told Lacey what had happened earlier that evening, as well as what he had experienced inside Eric's head—the memory of the scene at Caroline's house, with its overwhelming feelings of frustration and fear. Lacey listened for a bit, then paced around the shop. She materialized her fingers, and tried on a mask, turning to face Tristan for a moment, then trying on another.

"Maybe this isn't the first time Eric's gotten himself in deep," Lacey said. "What if Eric used to hit on Caroline for drug money—the way he now hits on Gregory? And what if that night, when he needed payment, Caroline didn't come through?"

"No, it's not that simple," Tristan replied, a little too quickly. "I know it's not that simple."

She raised an eyebrow at him. "You *know* that, or you just want to *believe* that?" she asked.

"What do you mean?"

"Seems to me you'd find it just a tiny bit satisfying to prove Gregory guilty. Poor, innocent, handsome Gregory," she said, baiting Tristan. "Maybe the only things he's guilty of are playing games with girls and falling for *your* girl—and your girl falling for him," she added slyly.

"You can't really believe that!" Tristan said.

She shrugged. "I'm not saying Gregory isn't a jerk sometimes, but other times, at least one time, he had a good enough heart to save the neck of his messed-up friend." She ran her tongue over her teeth and smiled. "I think he's rich, good-looking, and innocent."

"If he's innocent, his memory will prove it," Tristan said.

Lacey shook her head, suddenly serious. "This time he may throw you as far as the moon."

"I'll take my chances, and I'll succeed, Lacey. After all, I've had such an excellent teacher."

She squinted at him.

"You were right. Eric was easier to slip into when he was sleeping lightly. I'm going to try the same thing with Gregory."

"That will teach me not to teach you!"

Tristan cocked his head. "It ought to get you some points, Lacey—angel points for helping me complete my mission."

She turned away.

"And those points might help you finish yours. Isn't that what you want?"

Lacey shrugged, keeping her back turned to him.

Tristan looked at her, puzzled. "Is there something I don't get?"

"A lot, Tristan." She sighed. "What do you want me to do with this flower?"

"Leave it, I guess. It was nice of you to bring it, but I'll use up too much strength trying to carry it. Listen, I've got to get going."

She nodded.

"Thanks, Lacey."

She still didn't turn around.

"You're an angel!" he said.

"Mmm."

Tristan hurried off and arrived in Ivy's bedroom just as the sky was beginning to lighten. It was so tempting to materialize one finger and run it along her cheek.

I love you, Ivy. I've never stopped loving you.

Just one soft touch, that's all he wanted. What would it cost, one soft touch?

He left her before he gave in to the temptation and used up energy that he needed for Gregory.

Gregory was sleeping restlessly. Tristan looked quickly through his music collection and found a CD he was familiar with. Materializing two fingers, he slipped the disk into the player and turned the volume on low. He nudged Gregory, then he began to follow the music himself, saying the words, concentrating on the song's images.

But for some reason, Tristan kept getting mixed up. He'd thought he knew the lyrics by heart. He refocused, then realized his images were intermixing with other images—Gregory's.

I'm in! Lacey, I'm in!

Suddenly he could feel Gregory searching for him, reaching out blindly, desperately, the way a sleeper gropes for a clock when an alarm goes off. Tristan held himself still, absolutely still, and the music floated Gregory away from him.

Tristan sagged with relief. How far could Gregory blast him from his mind? he wondered.

But every thought like that was a thought different from Gregory's and would only alert him again. Tristan couldn't think about what he was doing but simply had to do it.

He had chosen to focus on the floor lamp in Caroline's living room. The day he and Lacey searched the house, he had noticed it standing next to the chair where the police had found Caroline's body. The halogen lamp, with its long pole and metal disk at the top, was so common it wouldn't create suspicion, but it might trigger a visual memory of Caroline sitting in the chair on that late-May afternoon.

Tristan focused on it. He circled it with his mind. He reached out for it as if he would switch it on.

And he found himself standing in Caroline's living room. She was sitting in the chair, looking back at him, slightly amused. Then she suddenly got up. The color was high in her cheeks, long red fingers of it, rising as it did in Gregory's cheeks when he was angry. But there was also a victorious gleam in her eyes.

She walked toward a desk. Tristan, inside Gregory's memory, stayed where he was, close to the lamp. Caroline picked up a piece of paper and waved it at him, as if she was taunting him. He felt Gregory's hands draw up into fists.

Then she walked toward him. He thought she was telling him to look at the paper, but he couldn't hear the words clearly. His anger had grown so quickly, the fury in him was so great, that his heart pounded, his blood rushed through him, singing in his ears.

Then his hand rose up. He slammed it into the lamp, slammed the lamp toward her. He saw her go reeling back, flying backward like a cartoon figure into the bright blue square of the picture window.

He shouted out. Tristan, himself, shouted out when he saw Caroline pitching backward, a long stripe of blood on her face.

181

Gregory suddenly jerked, and Tristan knew that Gregory had heard him. He was the one who'd get slammed next. He scrambled to get out. But images were swirling around him now like pieces of sharp, colored glass in a kaleidoscope. He felt dizzy and sick. He couldn't separate his own mind from Gregory's. He ran a maze through endless, circling, insane thoughts. He knew he was trapped.

Then suddenly there was a voice calling to Gregory, pleading with him to wake up. Ivy.

He saw her through Gregory's eyes, wrapped in her robe, leaning over him. Her hair tumbled down and touched his face. Her arms went around him, comforting him. Then Gregory stilled his whirling thoughts, and Tristan slipped out.

12

"That's it, Philip!" Gregory said, lifting up his shirt, wiping the sweat from his face. "I'm not giving you any more tennis lessons. You're going to beat me every time."

"Then I'll have to give *you* lessons," Philip replied, extremely pleased with himself.

Gregory finished taking off his damp shirt and swatted Philip lightly. "Brat."

Ivy and Maggie, who had been watching Thursday morning's lesson, laughed.

"This is how I'd always hoped it would be," Maggie said.

It was a perfect summer day, the sky postcard blue, the pine trees stirring with a light breeze. They were sitting together by the tennis court, Ivy sunbathing, her mother occupying the shady half of the blanket.

Maggie sighed contentedly. "We're a family at last! And I can go away knowing my chickens are happy and safe at home."

"Don't spend one moment thinking about us, Mom," Ivy said. "You and Andrew deserve some time alone at the lake."

Maggie nodded. "Andrew needs the time away, that's for sure. Something's been on his mind lately. Usually, before bed, he tells me everything that's happened that day—every detail of everything. That's how I get to sleep."

Ivy laughed.

"But I can tell," Maggie continued, "something's worrying him, and he's keeping it to himself."

Ivy laid her hand over her mother's. "You guys really need to get away from us and from the college, too. I hope you have a great time, Mom."

Her mother kissed her, then rose to say goodbye to Philip.

She put her arm around his shoulder. "You be good, pumpkin."

Philip made a face.

"Okay," Gregory answered cheerfully.

Maggie laughed. She planted a big, pink kiss on Philip, hesitated, then shyly kissed Gregory, too.

"Take care of my baby," Ivy heard her mother say quietly. "Take care of my big baby and my little one."

Gregory smiled. "You can count on me, Maggie."

Ivy's mother walked off happily, her huge pocketbook swinging behind her. The car was already packed; she was picking up Andrew after his morning meeting.

Gregory smiled down at Ivy, then stretched out on the blanket next to her. "For the next three days," he said, "we can eat whatever we want, whenever we want."

"I'm going to make a sandwich now," Philip told them. "Want one?"

Ivy shook her head. "I have to go to work soon. I'll pick up something at the mall."

"What kind are you making?" Gregory asked.

"Cream cheese, cinnamon, and sugar."

"Think I'll pass on that."

Philip started for the house, but not before wiping his face on his shirt, then pulling it off and swatting a tree with it.

When her brother had disappeared behind the grove of pines separating the house from the tennis court, Ivy said, "You know, he's imitating you. How do you like being a role model?"

"I don't know." Gregory smiled a lopsided smile. "I guess I'm going to have to clean up my act."

Ivy laughed and settled back on the blanket. "Thanks for being nice to my mom," she said.

"Promising to take care of her baby? That

won't be a hard one to keep." Gregory lay back close to Ivy. He glanced at her, then ran a light hand over her bare midriff. "Your skin's so warm."

Ivy felt warm all over. She laid her hand on top of Gregory's.

"How come you didn't wear that bikini to Eric's party?" he asked.

Ivy laughed. "I only wear it where I feel comfortable."

"And you're comfortable with me?" He pulled himself up on one elbow and looked into her eyes, then let his gaze pass slowly down her.

"Yes and no," she replied.

"You're always so honest," he said, bending over her, smiling.

Without touching her, he lowered his mouth to hers. She kissed him. He pulled up for a moment, then lowered his mouth again, still not touching her except with his lips.

They kissed a third time. Then Ivy reached up and slipped her hands around his neck, pulling him down to her.

She didn't hear the soft footsteps in the grass.

"I was waiting for you at the park since ten."

Gregory's head jerked up, and Ivy grabbed the edge of the blanket.

"Looks like you found something better to do," Eric said, and nodded at Ivy.

Gregory lifted himself off her. Ivy pulled the blanket around her, as if Eric had caught her without any clothes. The way he looked at her, she felt naked. She felt exposed.

Eric laughed.

"I saw a movie about a sister who couldn't keep her hands off her brother."

"It's *step*brother," Gregory told him.

Ivy huddled inside the blanket.

"Whatever. I guess you're over Tristan, huh?" Eric said. "Gregory's cured you?"

"Lay off, Eric," Gregory warned.

"Is he better at it than Tristan?" Eric asked, his voice low and soft. "He's sure got all the moves." His words were like snakes working their way into Ivy's mind.

"Shut up!" Gregory shouted, jumping to his feet.

"But you knew that, didn't you?" Eric continued in a silky voice. "You knew about Gregory because girls talk."

"Get out of here!"

"Suzanne would have told you," Eric went on.

"I'm warning you—"

"Suzanne would have told her best friend just how hot Gregory is," Eric said, wriggling his hips.

"Get off my property!"

Eric turned to Gregory and laughed. "*Your* property?" He stretched his lips into an exaggerated smile. "Yours? Maybe one day, *if* you're lucky."

Gregory was silent for a moment, then spoke with a voice that was cool but threatening. "You'd better hope I am, Eric. Because if I'm out of luck, you're out, too." He took several steps closer to his friend.

Eric took off. He looked over his shoulder and laughed, like a kid skipping away and daring others to catch him, but there was a maniacal edge to his laughter that made Ivy's blood run cold.

Philip, who had come out of the house when he heard the shouting, now raced across the lawn to them.

"What's wrong?" he asked. He looked from Gregory to Ivy, who was standing next to him, still wrapped in the blanket. "What happened?"

"Nothing," Gregory said. "Nothing for you to worry about."

Philip looked at him doubtfully, then turned to Ivy. "Are you okay?"

She nodded silently.

Gregory put his arm around Ivy. "Eric said some mean things to her."

"Mean things like what?"

"Just mean things," Gregory replied.

"Like what?"

"I don't want to talk about it right now," Ivy said.

Philip bit his lip. Then he turned and started to walk away from them.

Ivy knew that he felt left out. She slipped out from under Gregory's protective arm. "Can I have a hug, Philip? I know you're getting big now, but I'm feeling kind of bad. Can I have a hug?"

Her brother turned back and wrapped his arms around her, squeezing her tight.

"We'll take care of you," he whispered.

"Will you?" she whispered back.

"Gregory and me," he assured her, "and angel Tristan."

Ivy quickly let go of him. She tried hard to keep her mouth from quivering. "Thanks," she said, then ran into the house.

When Tristan heard the shouting, he rushed to the window to see what was going on. Gregory and Eric were hidden behind the trees. The sound of their voices carried, but he couldn't catch the words. The angry exchange was over almost as quickly as it had begun.

Tristan debated what to do. He wanted to make sure Ivy was all right, but he couldn't leave Gregory's bedroom as it looked now. He had spent the morning searching it, and drawers were still open, papers spread around, the pockets of pants and jackets pulled inside out. If Gregory discovered that someone had been looking through his things, he would become much more cautious, and that would make it harder to figure out what was going on.

The last time Ivy had needed help, she had called out to Tristan—silently—but he had heard her. He kept very still for a few moments now, listening. When he didn't sense that she was in danger, he decided to stay where he was and began to straighten up.

A few minutes later he heard Ivy running upstairs, then Philip and Gregory talking as they approached the house. Tristan began to work more quickly, but he was rapidly losing his strength. His fingers, having materialized repeatedly for short periods of time, were growing tired and clumsy. He could barely open and close Gregory's desk.

There was an old school magazine on top of the desk, anchoring newspaper articles Gregory had saved. Earlier, Tristan had skimmed the news stories, trying to figure out why they interested Gregory. Now they were blowing around. He snatched at one of them and knocked over a stack of boxes containing tapes for the VCR.

Several of the tapes slid out of their boxes, and Tristan hurried to pick them up. He could hear Gregory talking to Philip at the bottom of the back stairway, but the more he hurried, the more he bungled. One of the tapes wouldn't slip back into its box—something was sticking.

Tristan focused all his energy and yanked it out again. That's when he saw it, cellophane taped along one side of the black casing, with three bright red capsules inside.

He heard the steps creak. Gregory was coming up. Tristan ripped off the plastic, slid the tape back in its box, and set it on top of the stack. He knew that Gregory would not be able to see him, but he'd spot the red capsules. With his last bit of energy, Tristan threw them behind the bureau. A half second later Gregory entered the room.

Tristan sank back, exhausted. He saw that everything was in place except a train schedule that lay on the floor where the boxes had fallen.

No problem, he told himself. Gregory would think it had blown off the desk, since it wasn't anchored by anything.

In fact, Gregory didn't notice the schedule, though he went directly to his desk and sat down. There were beads of sweat on his forehead, and his skin had turned a strange color, paling beneath his tan. He dropped his head in his hands. For several minutes, he rubbed his temples, then he sat back in the chair.

Suddenly his head jerked around. Gregory

stared at the train schedule on the floor, then glanced slowly, suspiciously around the room. He reached for the videotape and pulled it out of the box. His jaw dropped.

He checked the label, then yanked out one tape after another. He ripped cellophane off a second cassette—it contained three more capsules—and again glanced around the room.

"Philip!" He stood up abruptly, knocking his chair back on the floor. He started for the door, then stopped and slammed his palm against the wall. He stood there, motionless, staring at the door to the hall, one hand still clutching the drugs.

"Damn you, brat!"

He shoved the capsules deep in his pocket, then slipped his wallet in after them. Returning to his desk, he picked up the chair, then sat down to read the train schedule.

Tristan read over his shoulder and watched as Gregory circled the time of the last train running after midnight. It left Tusset at 1:45 A.M., but didn't make a stop at Stonehill's little station. Gregory did some quick calculations, wrote down 2:04, circled it twice, then slipped the schedule under a book. He sat for fifteen minutes more, his chin resting on his hands.

Tristan wondered what was going through Gregory's mind, but he was much too weak to attempt an entrance. Gregory seemed much calmer now—so calm it was eerie. He sat back slowly and nodded to himself as if he had made some big decision. Then he reached for his car keys and started toward the door. Halfway down the steps, Gregory began to whistle.

"I think its blooming days are over," Beth said, eyeing the dead poppy that Ivy had placed in the water glass on the table between them.

When Lillian and Betty opened the shop Thursday morning, they had found the purple flower in King Kong's mouth, poking out like a rose between a dancer's teeth. Later that day Ivy had repeatedly denied being the joker who had placed it there.

"Why are we trying to revive it?" Beth asked. She swirled her tongue around her ice cream cone. "Can't we buy King Kong another one?"

"They were selling poppies at the festival Saturday," Ivy replied. "I bought some purple ones for Tristan. Philip and I took them to the cemetery."

"I'm glad Philip went with you," Beth said. "He misses Tristan, too."

"He made a *T* with them on the grave," Ivy told her, smiling a little.

Beth nodded, as if it were perfectly clear now why Ivy would bother with a wilted poppy left in the shop.

"I'm going crazy, aren't I?" Ivy said suddenly. "I'm supposed to be getting better! I'm supposed to be getting over Tristan! And here I am, saving this stupid flower like a souvenir because it looks like one that I—"

She plucked the poppy out of the glass and tossed it on a tray of dirty dishes that a waitress was carrying by.

Beth slipped out of the booth, chased down the waitress, and returned with the poppy.

"Maybe it will seed," she said, sticking it back in the water glass.

Ivy shook her head and sipped her tea in silence. Beth munched her cone for a few minutes.

"You know," Beth said at last, "I'm always prepared to listen."

Ivy nodded. "I'm sorry, Beth. I call you in a panic at nine o'clock at night, drag you away from your writing to get a snack with the over-fifty-but-still-swinging bowling league at Howard Johnson's"—she glanced around the crowded green and orange room—"and now I can't seem to talk."

"That's okay," Beth said, waving her cone at Ivy. "I'm having a triple dip of double fudge—for that, you could have called me at three in the morning. But how'd you know I was writing?"

Ivy smiled. Beth had met her in the parking lot wearing cutoff sweatpants, no makeup, and an old pair of glasses, which she wore only when she was glued to a computer screen. A scribbled note on a yellow Post-it was still stuck to her T-shirt, and her hair was pulled back in a binder clip.

"Just a hunch," Ivy said. "What's Suzanne up to tonight?"

Ivy and Suzanne had not spoken since the festival.

"She's out with somebody."

"Gregory?" Ivy asked, frowning. He had promised to stay with Philip till she got home that night.

"No, some guy who's supposed to make Gregory unbelievably jealous."

"Oh."

"She didn't tell you?" Beth asked with surprise. "That's all Suzanne could talk about." Seeing the look on Ivy's face, she added quickly, "I'm sure Suzanne thought she did. You know how it is— you say something to one person, and you think you've said it to the other."

Ivy nodded, but both of them knew that wasn't the case.

"Gregory hasn't spent much time with Suzanne lately," Beth said, pausing to chase drips of chocolate around her cone, "but you know that."

Ivy shrugged. "He goes out, but I don't ask him where."

"Well, Suzanne is sure he's seeing someone else."

Ivy began to trace the pictures on her place mat.

"At first Suzanne thought he was just playing around. She wasn't worried because it wasn't anyone special. But now she thinks he's seeing just one person. She thinks he's really hooked on somebody."

Ivy glanced up and saw Beth studying her. Can Beth actually read minds, she wondered, or is it my face that always gives me away?

"Suzanne keeps asking me what I think is going on," Beth continued, her brow slightly puckered.

"And what did you tell her?" Ivy asked.

Beth blinked several times, then looked away. She watched a silver-haired waitress flirt with two bald men in burgundy satin bowling shirts.

"I'm not a good person to ask," she said at last.

"You know me, Ivy, I'm always watching people and adding stuff to what I see to make stories out of them. Sometimes I forget what part I've made up and what part is really true."

"What do you think is really true about Gregory?" Ivy persisted.

Beth waved her cone around. "I think he gets around. I think that, uh, lots of different girls like him. But I can't guess who he's really interested in and what he's actually thinking. I just can't read him very well."

Beth took a crunching bite out of her cone and chewed thoughtfully. "Gregory's like a mirror," she said. "He reflects whoever he's with. When he's with Eric, he seems to act like Eric. When he's with you, he's thoughtful and funny like you. The problem for me is that I can't ever really see who Gregory is, any more than I can see what a mirror by itself looks like, because he reflects whoever's around him. Know what I mean?"

"I think I do."

"What should I say, Ivy?" Beth asked, the tone of her voice changing. She was pleading for an answer. "You're both my friends. When Suzanne asks me what's going on, what should I say?"

"I don't know." Ivy started examining her place mat again, reading all the descriptions of HoJo's desserts. "I'll tell you when I do know, okay? So, how's your writing going?"

"My writing?" Beth repeated, struggling to shift gears with Ivy. "Well, I've got good news."

"Yeah? Tell me."

"I'm going to be published. I mean, in a real magazine." Beth's blue eyes sparkled. *"True-Heart Confessions."*

"Beth, that's great! Which story?"

"The one I did for drama club. You know, it was in the lit mag at school last spring."

Ivy tried to recall it. "I've read so many now."

"'She clutched the gun to her breast,'" Beth began. "'Hard and blue, cold and unyielding. Photos of him. Frail and faded photos of him—of him with *her*—torn up, tear-soaked, salt-crusted photos,' et cetera, et cetera."

Two waitresses, carrying full trays, had stopped to listen.

"What is it?" Beth asked Ivy. "You've got a really funny look on your face."

"Nothing . . . nothing, I was just thinking," Ivy replied.

"You've been doing a lot of that lately."

Ivy laughed. "Maybe I can keep it up next month when school starts."

Their check was dropped on the table. Ivy reached for her purse.

"Listen," Beth said, "why don't you sleep over

at my house tonight? We don't have to talk. We'll watch videos, polish our nails, bake cookies . . ." She popped the tip of her sugar cone into her mouth. "Low-cal cookies," she added.

Ivy smiled, then began digging in her purse for money. "I should get home, Beth."

"No, you shouldn't."

Ivy stopped digging. Beth had spoken with such certainty.

"I don't know why," Beth said, twisting a piece of her hair self-consciously. "You just shouldn't."

"I have to be home," Ivy told her. "If Philip wakes up in the middle of the night and finds I'm not there, he'll think something's wrong."

"Call him," her friend replied. "If he's asleep, Gregory can leave a note by his bed. You shouldn't go home tonight. It's . . . a feeling, a really strong feeling I have."

"Beth, I know you get these feelings, and one time before you were right, but this time it's different. The doors will be locked. Gregory is home. Nothing is going to happen to me."

Beth was looking past Ivy's shoulder, her eyes narrowing as if she was trying to focus on something.

Ivy turned around quickly and saw a curly-haired man in a shiny yellow bowling shirt. He winked at her, and Ivy turned back.

"Can I stay over with you?" Beth asked.

"What? No. Not tonight," Ivy said. "I need some sleep, and you need to finish that story I interrupted. This was my treat," she added, scooping up the check.

In the parking lot Ivy said good-bye several times, and Beth left her reluctantly.

As Ivy drove home she thought about Beth's story. The details of Caroline's suicide had not been made public, so Beth didn't know about the photos that Caroline had torn up the day she shot herself. It was funny the way Beth came up with things in her writing that seemed farfetched and kind of melodramatic, until some version of them came true.

When Ivy arrived home, she saw that all the lights in the house were out except one, a lamp in Gregory's room. She hoped he hadn't noticed her car coming up the drive. She left it outside the garage. That way, if he got worried, he could see that she had arrived home safely. Ivy planned to go up the center stairs so she wouldn't have to pass his room. In the afternoon Gregory had called the shop twice. She knew he wanted to talk, and she wasn't ready.

It was a warm evening, with no moon up yet, only stars sequining the sky. Ivy gazed up at them for a few moments, then walked quietly across the grass and patio.

"Where have you been?"

She jumped. She hadn't seen him sitting in the shadow of the house.

"What?"

"Where have you been?"

Ivy prickled at his tone. "Out," she said.

"You should have called me back. Why didn't you call me back, Ivy?"

"I was busy with customers."

"I thought you'd come home right after work."

Ivy dropped her keys noisily onto a cast-iron table. "And I thought I wouldn't be questioned about going out for an hour—not by you. I'm getting tired of it, Gregory!"

She could hear him shifting in the chair, but couldn't see his face.

"I'm getting tired of everyone watching out for me! Beth isn't my mother, and *you're* not my big brother!"

He laughed softly. "I'm glad to hear you say that. I was afraid that Eric had gotten you mixed up."

Ivy dropped her head a little, then said, "Maybe he did." She took a step toward the house.

Gregory caught her wrist. "We need to talk."

"I need to think, Gregory."

"Then think out loud," he said.

She shook her head.

"Ivy, listen to me. We're not doing anything wrong."

"Then why do I feel so—so confused? And so disloyal?"

"To Suzanne?" he asked.

"Suzanne thinks you're seeing someone else," Ivy told him.

"I am," he replied quietly. "I'm just not sure if she's seeing me. . . . Are you?"

Ivy bit her lip. "It isn't just Suzanne I'm thinking of."

"Tristan."

She nodded.

He tugged on her arm, pulling her closer to him. "Sit down."

"Gregory, I don't want to talk about it."

"Then just listen. Hear me out. You love Tristan. You love him like you love no one else."

Ivy pulled away a little, but he held her fingers tightly. "Listen! If you had been the one killed in the accident, what would you have wanted for Tristan? Would you want no one else to love him? Would you want him to be alone the rest of his life?"

"No, of course not," she said.

"Of course not," he repeated softly.

Then he pulled her down into the chair with him. The metal was cold and hard.

"I've been thinking about you all day and all night," he said.

He caressed her lightly, his fingers tracing her face and the bones of her neck. He kissed her as gently as he would a child. She let him, but she didn't kiss him back.

"I've been waiting here all night," he said. "I need to get out. How about going for a ride with me?"

"We can't leave Philip," Ivy reminded him.

"Sure we can," Gregory replied softly. "He's sound asleep. We'll lock up the house and turn on the outside alarm. We can drive around for a little while. And I won't talk any more, promise."

"We can't leave Philip," she said a second time.

"He'll be all right. There's nothing wrong with riding around, Ivy. There's nothing wrong with blasting the stereo and driving a little fast. There's nothing wrong with having a good time."

"I don't want to go," she said.

She felt his body go rigid.

"Not tonight," she added quickly. "I'm tired, Gregory. I really need to go to bed. Another night, maybe."

"All right. Whatever you want," he said, his voice husky. He sagged back against the chair. "Get some sleep."

Ivy left him there and felt her way through the

dark house. She checked on Philip, then walked through the adjoining bath to her own bedroom, where she was greeted by Ella's glowing eyes. Ivy switched on a small bureau lamp, and Ella began to purr.

"Is that purr for me," Ivy asked, "or him?"

Tristan's picture, the one his mother had given her, sat within the yellow circle of light.

Ivy took the picture in her hands. Tristan smiled up at her, wearing his old baseball cap—backward, of course. His school jacket flapped open, as if he were walking toward her. Sometimes she still couldn't believe that he was dead. Her head knew that he was, knew that in one sudden moment Tristan had stopped existing, but her heart just wouldn't let go.

"Love you, Tristan," she said, then kissed the photograph. "Sweet dreams."

Ivy woke up screaming. Her voice was hoarse, as if she had been screaming for hours. The clock said 1:15 A.M.

"It's okay! You're safe! Everything's okay, Ivy."

Gregory had his arms around her. Philip stood next to the bed, clutching Ella.

Ivy stared at them, then sank back against Gregory. "When will it stop? When will this nightmare end?"

"Shh, shh. Everything's okay."

But it wasn't. The nightmare kept growing. It kept adding on details, continually sending out tendrils of fear that curled into the dark places of her mind. Ivy closed her eyes, resting her head against Gregory.

"Why does she keep dreaming?" Philip asked.

"I'm not sure," Gregory said. "I guess it's part of getting over the accident."

"Sometimes dreams are messages from angels," Philip suggested. He said *angels* quickly, then glanced at Ivy, as if he thought she'd yell at him for mentioning them again.

Gregory studied Philip for a moment, then asked, "Angels are good, aren't they?"

Philip nodded.

"Well, if angels are good," Gregory reasoned, "do you think they'd be sending Ivy bad dreams?"

Philip thought about it, then slowly shook his head. "No . . . but maybe it's a bad angel doing it."

Ivy felt Gregory stiffen.

"It's just my mind doing it," she said quietly. "It's just my mind getting used to what happened to Tristan and me. In a while, the nightmares will stop."

But she was lying. She was afraid the dreams would never stop. And she was starting to think that there was something more to them than her getting over Tristan's death.

"I have an idea, Philip," Gregory said. "Until Ivy's nightmares stop, we'll take turns waking her up and staying with her. Tonight's my turn. Next time it's yours, okay?"

Philip looked doubtfully from Gregory to Ivy. "Okay," he said at last. "Ivy, can I take Ella in my room?"

"Sure. She'd love to cuddle with you."

Ivy watched her brother as he carried Ella, his head bent over her, his brow furrowed.

"Philip," she called after him. "When I get home from work tomorrow, we'll do something, just you and me. Think about what you want it to be—something fun. Everything's all right Philip. Really. Everything will be all right."

He nodded, but she could tell that he didn't believe her.

"Sleep tight," Ivy said. "You've got Ella with you. And your angel," she added.

He looked at her, his eyes wide with surprise. "You saw him, too?"

Ivy hesitated.

"Of course not," Gregory answered for her.

Of course not, Ivy repeated to herself—and yet for a moment she almost thought she did. She could almost believe an angel existed for Philip, though not for herself.

"Good night," she said softly.

When he was gone, Gregory held Ivy close to

him and rocked her for several minutes. "Same old dream?" he said.

"Yes."

"Is Eric still in it?"

"The red motorcycle is," Ivy replied.

"I wish I could stop your nightmares," Gregory said. "If I knew how, I'd dream them myself every night. If only I could keep you from going through this."

"I don't think anyone can stop them," she replied.

He lifted his head. "What do you mean?"

"There was something new tonight. The same way the motorcycle got added on before, something else was added this time. Gregory, I think I might be remembering things. And I think I might have to keep doing this until I remember—something." She shrugged.

He pulled his head back a little to look at her. "What was added to the dream?"

"I was driving. The window was there, the one I can't quite see through with the shadow on the other side. It was that same window, but this time I was driving toward it, not walking."

She paused. She didn't want to think about it, think what the new part could mean.

He held her close again. "And everything else was the same?"

"No. I was driving Tristan's car."

Ivy heard the sharp intake of breath.

"When I saw the window, I tried to stop the car. I stepped on the brake, but the car wouldn't slow down. Then I heard his voice. 'Ivy, stop! Stop! Don't you see, Ivy? Ivy, stop!' But I couldn't stop. I couldn't slow down. I pressed down the pedal over and over. I had no brakes!"

Ivy felt cold all over. Gregory's arms were around her, but his own skin was cold with sweat.

"Why were there no brakes?" she whispered. "Am I remembering, Gregory? *What* am I remembering?"

He didn't answer. He was shaking as much as she.

"Stay with me," she begged. "I'm afraid to go back to sleep."

"I'll stay, but you have to sleep, Ivy."

"I can't! I'm afraid I'll start dreaming again. It frightens me! I don't know what will happen next!"

"I'll be right here. I'll wake you as soon as you start dreaming, but you need to sleep. I'll get you something to help you."

He stood up.

"Where are you going?" she asked, panicky.

"Shh," he soothed. "I'm just going to fix you something to help you sleep."

Then he took Tristan's photo down from the bureau and set it on the night table next to her.

"I'll be right back. I won't leave you, Ivy, I promise I won't leave you." He smoothed her hair. "Not until these nightmares stop for good."

14

"Ivy, stop! Stop! Don't you see, Ivy? Ivy, stop!"

But she hadn't stopped. Ivy kept telling Gregory the dream, and now he knew that she was remembering more. Maybe next time she'd remember it all—whatever it was Gregory didn't want anyone to know. If there was a next time.

Tristan lay still in Ivy's room. He had gone crazy, shouting and screaming at her. He had used up huge amounts of energy. For what? She sat fidgeting, frightened—and hoping for Gregory's return.

Tristan pulled himself up. He rushed out of the bedroom and down the main stairway of the darkened house, turning instinctively toward the kitchen, where Gregory was. Only the small light over the stove was on. Water hissed in the teapot.

Gregory sat on a stool at the counter, watching it, his skin pale and glistening.

He kept toying with a cellophane packet he had taken from his pocket. Tristan could guess what it contained and what Gregory planned to do next. And he knew that, even if he had his full strength now, he couldn't overcome him. He couldn't use Gregory's mind the way he could use Will's. Gregory would fight Tristan all the way, and his human body had a physical strength a hundred times greater than that of Tristan's materialized fingers.

But human fingers could still slip, Tristan thought. If a little red capsule—something that Tristan could manipulate—moved unexpectedly, Gregory might fumble.

Gregory had chosen raspberry tea, perhaps because its sharp flavor would cover the taste of a drug, Tristan thought. He moved steadily closer to Gregory. He'd have to materialize his fingers at just the right moment.

Gregory carefully undid the cellophane packet and picked up two of the three capsules. Tristan extended his glowing hand and began to focus on his fingertips. Gregory's hand hovered over the hot tea.

The moment he let go, Tristan flicked the capsules away. They skittered across the countertop. Gregory swore and flung out his hand, but

Tristan was quicker and flicked them into the sink. The capsules stuck to the damp surface and Tristan had to work again to get them down the drain.

As he did Gregory dropped the third capsule into the tea.

Now Tristan reached for the mug, but Gregory wrapped his fingers firmly around it. He stirred the liquid with a spoon, and when the capsule had dissolved, he carried the cup upstairs.

Ivy looked so relieved to see him.

"This ought to help," Gregory said.

"Don't drink it, Ivy!" Tristan warned, though he knew she couldn't hear him.

She sipped, then set it down and laid her head against Gregory.

He picked the cup up again before Tristan could touch it. "Too hot?"

"No, it's good. Thank you."

"Stop!" Tristan cried.

She sipped again, as if to reassure Gregory that the tea was fine.

"I chose the right stuff, didn't I? You've got so many kinds down there."

"Put it down, Ivy."

"It's perfect," she said, and took longer drinks.

"Lacey, where are you when I need you? I need your voice, I need someone to tell her no!"

Whenever Ivy reached to put the drugged tea back on the table, Gregory took it from her and held it. He sat on the bed with her, one arm around her, the other lifting the cup to her lips.

"A little more," he coaxed.

"No more!" Tristan cried.

"How do you feel?" he asked several minutes later.

"Sleepy. Strange. Not scared . . . just strange. I feel like someone else is here, watching us," she said, glancing around the room.

"I'm here, Ivy!"

Gregory offered her the last mouthful of tea. "There's nothing to be worried about," he said. "I'm here for you, Ivy."

Tristan struggled to keep himself calm. One capsule probably wouldn't kill her, he reasoned. Had Gregory found the other pack that Tristan had thrown behind the bureau? Was he planning to dope her up a little, then give her the rest?

"Lacey, I can't save her by myself!"

Will, Tristan thought, find Will. But how long would that take? Ivy's eyes were slowly closing.

"Sleep," Gregory was saying over and over. "There's nothing to be afraid of. Sleep."

Ivy's eyes shut, then her head dropped. Gregory did not bother to catch her. He pushed her to the side and let her slump against the pillow.

Without realizing it, Tristan had begun to cry. He wrapped his arms around Ivy, though he could not hold her. She was far away from him, and drifting away from Gregory, too, sinking further and further into an unnatural sleep. Tristan cried helplessly.

Gregory got up abruptly and walked out of the room.

Tristan knew he had to get help, but he couldn't leave Ivy alone for long.

Philip. It was his only chance. Tristan hurried into the next room.

Ella became alert as soon as he entered.

"Help me out, Ella. We need to get him awake, just enough to let me in."

Ella climbed up on Philip's chest, sniffed at his face, then mewed.

Philip's eyes fluttered open. His small hand reached up and lazily scratched Ella. Tristan imagined how soft the cat felt to Philip. A second later, having shared his thoughts, he slipped inside the boy.

"It's me, Philip. Your friend, your angel, Tristan."

"Tristan," Philip murmured, and suddenly they were sitting across from each other with a checkerboard between them. Philip jumped Tristan's marker. "Crown me!"

Tristan had dropped into a memory or a

dream woven from a memory. He struggled to get them out of it.

"Wake up, Philip. It's Tristan. Wake up. I need your help. Ivy needs your help."

Tristan could hear Ella purring again and saw her face peering into his, though everything was blurry. He knew Philip was listening and waking up slowly.

"Come on, Philip. That's the way, buddy."

Philip was looking over at the angel statues now. He was wondering, but he was not afraid. His arms and legs still felt relaxed. So far, so good.

Then Tristan heard the noise in the hall. He heard footsteps—Gregory's—but Gregory was walking oddly, heavily.

"Get up, Philip! We have to see!"

Before Philip could rouse himself, Gregory was down the stairs. A moment later, an outside door banged.

"Put on your shoes. Your shoes!"

A car's engine sputtered. Tristan recognized it—Ivy's old Dodge. His heart sank. Gregory had Ivy with him. Where are you taking her? Where?

"I don't know," Philip said in a sleepy voice.

Think. What would be easy for him? Tristan said to himself.

"I don't know," Philip mumbled.

218

With Ivy drugged, it would be easy to stage an accident. What kind? How and where was he going to do it? There must have been clues in his room, a hint in the newspaper clippings.

Tristan suddenly remembered the train schedule. He recalled the strange look on Gregory's face when he found the timetable on the floor. Gregory had circled the late-night train, the one that stopped at Tusset. Then he had done some calculations, written down a time, and circled it twice. 2:04. That would be right—Tristan knew the train rushed through their station a few minutes after two each morning. Rushed through! It didn't stop at small stations such as Stonehill's, which would be deserted after midnight. They had to stop him!

He glanced at Philip's digital clock. 1:43 A.M.

"Philip, come on!"

The little boy was slumped down in the chair, with only one shoelace tied. His fingers were clumsy when he tried to tie the other one. He could barely stand up, and moved slowly down the hall with Tristan guiding him. Tristan chose the center staircase, where there was a railing to hang on to. They made it safely to the bottom, then Tristan guided him around to the back door, which Gregory had left open. As if he had a clock inside him, Tristan felt each second ticking away.

They'd never make it in time by foot; the long driveway down the ridge took them in the opposite direction from the station. Keys—could he find the keys for Gregory's car? If he did, he could materialize his fingers and— But what if they wasted all their time looking for keys that Gregory had with him?

"Other way, Philip." Tristan turned Philip around. It was a dangerous shortcut, but their only chance: the steep and rocky side of the ridge, which dropped to the station below.

After a couple of steps, the cool night air revived Philip. Through the boy's eyes and ears, Tristan became aware of the night's silvery shadows and rustling sounds. He too was feeling stronger. At Tristan's urging, Philip broke into a run across the grass. They raced past the tennis court, then forty yards more toward the boundary of the property, the edge where the land suddenly dropped off.

They were moving faster than a child could have, their powers combined. Tristan didn't know how long his renewed strength would hold out, and he wasn't certain that he could get them safely down the steep side of the ridge. It seemed to have taken forever just to get this far.

He felt a moment of resistance as he and Philip climbed the stone wall marking the end of the property.

"I'm not supposed to," Philip said.

"It's okay, you're with me."

Far below them he could see the train station. To get to it they'd have to climb down a hillside where the only toeholds were the roots of a few dwarfed trees and some narrow ledges of stone, with sheer drops beneath them. Occasionally patches of brush broke through the rocky surface, but mostly it was rutted earth with a cascade of tumbled rocks that would roll at the lightest touch of a foot.

"I'm not scared," Philip said.

"I'm glad that one of us isn't."

They picked their way slowly and carefully down the ridge. The moon had come up late and its shadows were long and confusing. Tristan had to continually check himself, reminding himself that the legs he was using were shorter, the arms unable to reach as far.

They were halfway down when he misjudged. Their jump was too short, and they leaned out too far from a narrow strip of rock. From their ledge, it was a straight drop down twenty-five feet, with nothing but stones to snag them at the bottom before another drop. They teetered. Tristan drew into himself, cloaking his thoughts and instincts, letting Philip take over. It was Philip's natural sense of balance that saved them.

As they descended, Tristan tried not to think

about Ivy, though the image of her head hanging over her shoulder like a limp doll's kept passing through his mind. And all the while he was aware of time ticking away.

"What is it?" Philip asked, sensing Tristan's concern.

"Keep going. Tell you later."

Tristan couldn't let Philip know how much danger Ivy was in. He cloaked certain thoughts, hiding from Philip's consciousness both Gregory's identity and his intentions. He wasn't sure how Philip would handle the information, whether he'd panic over Ivy or even try to defend Gregory.

They were at the bottom now, racing through the tall grass and weeds, getting tripped up by rocks. Philip's ankle twisted, but he kept going. Ahead of them was a high wire fence. Through it they saw the station.

The station had two tracks side by side, northbound and southbound, each with its own platform. The platforms were connected by a high bridge over the tracks. On the southbound side, which was farthest from Philip and Tristan, there was a wooden station house and a parking lot. Tristan knew that the late-night train ran southbound.

Just as they reached the fence Tristan heard the bells of a town church, tolling once, twice. Two o'clock.

"The fence is awfully high, Tristan."

"At least it's not electric."

"Can we rest?"

Before Tristan could answer, a train whistle sounded in the distance.

"Philip, we have to beat the train!"

"Why?"

"We have to. Climb!"

Philip did, digging his toes into the holes of the wire mesh, stretching and grasping with his fingers, pulling himself up. They were at the top of the fence, twenty feet high. Then Philip jumped. They slammed into the ground and rolled.

"Philip!"

"I thought you had wings. You're supposed to have wings."

"Well, *you* don't!" Tristan reminded him.

The whistle blew again, closer this time. They ran for the first platform. When they climbed up on it, they could see across the station.

Ivy.

"Something's wrong with her," Philip said.

She was standing on the southbound platform, leaning back against a pillar that was at the edge of the platform. Her head was hanging to one side.

"She could fall! Tristan, a train's coming and—" Philip began to shout. "Ivy! Ivy!"

She didn't hear him.

"The steps," Tristan told him.

They raced for them, then across the bridge and down the other side.

They could hear the train rumbling, getting closer. Philip kept calling to her, but Ivy stared across the track, mesmerized. Tristan followed her gaze—then he and Philip froze.

"Tristan? Tristan, where are you?" Philip asked in a panicky voice.

"Here. Right here. I'm still inside you."

But even to Tristan it looked as if he were out there, on the other side of the track. Tristan stared at the image of himself that stood in the shadows of the northbound platform. The strange figure was dressed in a school jacket, like the one Tristan wore in his photograph, and had an old baseball cap pulled on backward. Tristan stared, as entranced by the figure as Ivy and Philip.

"That's not me," he told Philip. "Don't be fooled. It's someone else dressed like me." Gregory, he said to himself.

"Who is it? Why's he dressed like you?"

They saw a pale hand move out of the shadows into the clear moonlight. The figure beckoned to Ivy, encouraging her, drawing her across the track.

The train was rushing toward them now, its headlight whitening the track beneath them, its whistle blasting in a final warning.

Ivy paid no attention to it. She was drawn to the hand like a moth to a flickering fire. It kept reaching out to her. She suddenly reached out her own hand and took a step forward.

"*Ivy!*" Tristan shouted—Philip shouted. "*Ivy! Ivy, don't!*"

Don't miss the thrilling continuation of

KISSED ᵇʸ ᴬᴺ ANGEL

Volume III:
Soulmates

Ella followed Ivy and leaped up in the dormer window across the room from Ivy's piano. Ivy sat down and began to work through her scales, sending out ripples of music. As her hands moved up and down the keyboard, she thought about Tristan, the way he'd looked when he swam with her, light scattered in the water drops around him, the way his light could shine around her now.

The late sunlight of September was a pure gold like his, and the sunset would have the same rim of colors. Ivy glanced toward the window and stopped playing abruptly. Ella was sitting up, her ears alert, her eyes big and shiny. Ivy turned quickly to look behind her. "Tristan," she said softly.

The glow surrounded her.

"Tristan," she whispered again. "Talk to me. Why can't I hear you? Can't you speak to me?"

But the only sound was the light thump of Ella as she leaped down from her perch and trotted over to them. Ivy wondered if the cat could see him.

"Yes, she saw me the first time I came."

Ivy was stunned by his voice. "It's you. You really are—"

"Amazing, isn't it?"

Within herself, Ivy could hear not only his voice but the laughter in it, sounding just as he always had when something amused him. Then the laughing ceased.

"Ivy, I love you. I'll never stop loving you."

Ivy laid her face down in her hands. Her palms and fingers were bathed in pale, golden light. "I love you, Tristan, and I've missed you. You don't know how much I've missed you."

"You don't know how often I've been with you, watching you sleep, listening to you play. It was like last winter all over again, waiting and wanting, hoping you'd notice me."

The yearning in his voice made Ivy quiver inside, the way his kisses once had. "I wish we'd had this summer together. I wish we could have floated side by side in the center of the lake, letting the sun sparkle at our fingers and toes."

"All I want is to be close to you," Tristan told her.

Ivy lifted her head. "I wish I could feel your arms around me."

"You couldn't get any closer to my heart than you are now." Ivy held out her arms, then folded them around herself like closed wings. "I've wished a thousand times I could tell you that I love you. But I never believed, I just never believed I'd be given a chance—"

"You have to believe, Ivy!" She heard the fear in his voice ringing inside her. "Don't stop believing, or you'll stop seeing me. You need me now, in ways that you don't know," he warned.

"Because of Gregory," she said, dropping her hands in her lap. "I do know. I just don't understand why he would want to"—she backed away from the most terrifying thought—"to hurt me."

"To *kill* you," said Tristan.

About the Author

Elizabeth Chandler has written picture books, chapter books, middle grade novels, and young adult romances under a variety of names. She lives in Baltimore, and loves stories, cats, baseball, and Bob—not necessarily in that order.

What's it like to be a witch?

Sabrina
The Teenage Witch™

"I'm 16, I'm a witch,
and I **still** have to go to school?"

◆◆◆◆◆

#1 Sabrina, the Teenage Witch
by David Cody Weiss and Bobbi JG Weiss

#2 Showdown at the Mall
by Diana G. Gallagher

#3 Good Switch, Bad Switch
by David Cody Weiss and Bobbi JG Weiss

#4 Halloween Havoc
by Diana Gallagher

#5 Santa's Little Helper
by Cathy East Dubowski

Based on the hit TV series

Look for a new title every other month.

From Archway Paperbacks
Published by Pocket Books

1345-04

For everyone who believes—
a romantic and suspenseful
new trilogy

KISSED BY AN ANGEL

by Elizabeth Chandler

When Ivy loses her boyfriend, Tristan, in a car
accident, she also loses her faith in angels. But
Tristan is now an angel himself, desperately
trying to protect Ivy. Only the power of love can
save her...and set her free to love again.

Volume I

Kissed by an Angel

Volume II

The Power of Love

Volume III

Soulmates

Available from Archway Paperbacks
Published by Pocket Books   1110-01